I0451072

AFTER YOU'VE GONE

AND OTHER OUTRÉ TALES

AFTER YOU'VE GONE

AND OTHER OUTRÉ TALES

JOHN PEYTON COOKE

**Éditions
Cuir Noir**
London

cuirnoir.com

This book is for
KENG

"After You've Gone" first appeared in *Stranger: Dark Tales of Eerie Encounters* (HarperCollins, New York, 2002). Copyright © 2002 by John Peyton Cooke.

"A Doll's Tale" first appeared in *Weird Tales* No. 295, Winter 1989/90. Copyright © 1989 by the Terminus Publishing Company, Inc.

"The Penitent" first appeared in *Dark Love* (ROC Books, New York, 1995). Copyright © 1995 by John Peyton Cooke.

"The Naked Tooth" first appeared in *Christopher Street* No. 185, August 17, 1992. Copyright © 1992 by That New Magazine, Inc.

"The Cat's Meow" first appeared in *Eldritch Tales* No. 12, 1986. Copyright © 1986 by Yith Press.

"Spoiled Rotten" first appeared in *Eldritch Tales* No. 28, 1993. Copyright © 1993 by Yith Press.

"Telling Tales" first appeared online at *The Mystery Zone*, October 1995. Copyright © 1995 by John Peyton Cooke.

"The Strawberry Man" first appeared in *Embracing the Dark* (Alyson Publications, Boston, 1991). Copyright © 1991 John Peyton Cooke.

"Sweet Chariot" first appeared in *Space & Time* No. 72, Summer 1987. Copyright © 1987 by Space & Time.

"Serostatus" first appeared in *The Magazine of Fantasy & Science Fiction* No. 624, January 2004. Copyright © 2003 by Spilogale, Inc.

Éditions Cuir Noir
J. P. Cooke, Publisher
113 St. George's Square, GFF
London SW1V 3QP United Kingdom
Web: www.cuirnoir.com
Web: www.johnpeytoncooke.com
E-mail: johnpeytoncooke@gmail.com
Twitter: @johnpeytoncooke

Contents

———

PREFACE

———

THE TALES IN THIS VOLUME represent all of my published short fiction as of this writing. I've assembled them for the pleasure of my readers, who might otherwise find it tedious to track down the original publications, some of them in rather obscure sources.

I like referring to these specimens as *outré* tales, as it may be the only apt descriptor that applies to each of them. They range from ghost stories, to grand guignol, to psychological suspense, to the surreal, to the campy and the quirky. Anyone who's read my work knows that I am always keen to showcase gay characters and what might be described as a gay point of view, but merely to describe these as *gay* tales would be somewhat misleading. These tales are really *out there*, in one respect or another, so the term *outré* seems most fitting.

This collection has come about because of the ease with which one can publish one's own work, via print-on-demand and e-books, as certainly no old-fashioned publisher would be the slightest bit interested in trying to figure out how to market this book to my invisible readership.

The act of putting it together has afforded me the opportunity to revisit these tales, the earliest of which, "The Cat's Meow," was written when I was sixteen, and the most recent of which, "Serostatus," when I was in my mid-thirties. Although they differ greatly in approach, subject matter, and literary *genre,* I find it personally intriguing to discern the commonalities amongst them and to discover that, taken as a whole, they credibly represent my creative personality in a naked and honest fashion. Certainly, anyone who has read my novels, such as *Torsos* and *The Chimney Sweeper,* would not be surprised by any of the eccentricities herein. And it is to be hoped that in reading these tales my audience will be amused, shocked, disturbed, touched . . . but above all entertained in some way.

Readers seeking specific notes relating to these tales are referred to the Afterword at the end of the volume.

Finally, if you do enjoy this book, please do not hesitate to let me know via e-mail at johnpeytoncooke@gmail.com.

John Peyton Cooke
London
7 July 2011

After You've Gone

———

I LOVED IT SO MUCH I was cradling it in my hands, fondling its stock, bracing its chamber between my thumbs, staring into its barrel like you'd look into a lover's eyes, in search of some kind of truth. It stared back at me deeply and gave me the ultimate truth: *Yeah, you got it right, Grant. I'm your trusty Glock. You can count on me. I'm going to kill you.*

I kissed its muzzle. My tongue tasted oil, and I could smell powder traces on my fingers. I'd cleaned it out after being down at the firing range all afternoon, blasting at all those black hanging targets, trying to get rid of all my black thoughts but only making them blacker. It was all I could do to keep from turning my Glock on myself then and there.

I didn't want to go out that way, in front of everybody. I wanted to have some privacy and leave a note—three notes, maybe, addressed to different people and taped up on my bathroom mirror. One to my landlord, saying sorry about the mess and take what you want. Another to Captain Fe-liciano, telling him thanks for your support when the going got tough, but face the facts, guy, I'm a screw-up. The last to Mom, saying love you lots and none of this is your fault, even if you did put Poncho to sleep.

I loved my Glock so much I was laying four of its six inches on my tongue, forming my lips around it, hooking my thumbs around its safe-action trigger. There's no such thing as a safety catch on a Glock—you have to apply direct pressure in the right spot, or the trigger acts like a safety and refuses to fire.

My thumb was in the right spot. The rest ought to be cake.

I was telling myself that if I was a real man, I'd do it.

I was sweating bullets, staring down at the trigger cross-eyed. The last thing I'd see would be the knuckle creases on my thumb parting ever so slightly.

I depressed the safe action so it wouldn't be safe anymore—and I wouldn't be depressed anymore.

I did it. I squeezed the trigger.

It should have fired. But it didn't. It jammed on me.

For the first time in my career, my Glock had let me down.

And now my hands were shaking and my heart was beating so fast I thought I was going to have a heart attack. If I tried again, I was going to screw it up. And I didn't want to fail.

I set the gun down. My stomach churned in disgust. With fumbling fingers, I tapped out a cigarette and lit it on the third match. It felt good to have that smoke in my lungs. The nicotine got my mind to thinking—maybe the ol' Glock was giving me a sign, that I needed help, that something was terribly wrong with me. And you don't argue with a Glock.

I didn't know where to begin. The brass always encouraged us to use the departmental psychiatrists—but everyone knew what that was about. I couldn't count on total confidentiality. Whatever was wrong with me might get leaked to IA. It might get subpoenaed in some future court case if my policing skills were called into question, and such a case was not outside the realm of possibility. It might simply get spread around as interprecinct gossip: *Officer Grant's a loose cannon. Yeah, you can't trust Tom Grant as your backup. The guy's nuts. Let's find him a nice desk job and pull him off the streets.*

I couldn't turn to the department. No, sir, not on my life.

Facedown on the kitchen table in front of me lay the *Village Voice*. One of the classified ads on the back page caught my eye:

> LONELY? DEPRESSED? SUICIDAL?
> CALL THE 24-HOUR HELP LINE!
> 555-HELP   555-HELP   555-HELP

It looked like what I needed. Help was only a phone call away. Even though it was two in the morning, somebody would be there on the other end of the line to talk me down.

I picked up the phone and called.

"Hello?" A man's voice, exceedingly mild, somewhat sleepy.

"Um, yes, is this the help line?" I croaked.

"Yeah, sure." He cleared his throat. "How can I help

you?"

"I—I just tried to kill myself."

"Really?"

"Yes, really."

"What happened? Why didn't it work?"

"My gun jammed."

"Oh, you're using a gun? What kind?"

"What kind? Does it matter?"

"Of course it matters. What kind of gun do you own?"

"Well, it's a Glock."

"Mmm," said the guy on the help line. "What model?"

"It's a seventeen-L. Semi-auto, six-inch barrel."

"What does that use? Nine-millimeters? Forty-caliber Smith & Wessons? Or forty-fives?"

"Nine-millimeters," I said.

"How many in the clip?"

"I've got seventeen in the clip and one in the chamber. The one in the chamber jammed. I'm going to have to start all over."

"How much does a gun like that cost?" the help line wanted to know.

"I don't know what it costs now. I got mine, what, four years ago, when I joined the academy. It set me back about eight hundred."

"The academy?" he said. "You mean the police academy?"

"Yes, I'm a policeman."

"How interesting."

"Listen, I'm serious about this. I'm going to take my Glock apart, clean it all up, reload it, and try again. Probably one chance in a billion that it'll jam again."

"Probably," the help line said.

There was an uncomfortable silence.

"Aren't you going to try to talk me out of it?"

"Why should I?"

"I thought that's what you were there for."

"If you want to kill yourself, and you thought I was going to try to talk you out of it, why would you call?" he asked.

"I don't follow," I said.

"Why don't you do it right now, while I'm on the phone?"

"What?"

"You heard me. Talk to me while you're unjamming your gun or whatever it is you have to do. I'll wait. Get it all nice and ready, and then do it. Just do it. I want to hear it."

"Listen, maybe I dialed the wrong number, buddy."

"No, you didn't. You dialed five-five-five-H-E-L-P, didn't you? That's me. I'm the help line. You got what you wanted."

"I still don't understand."

"Who cares whether you understand? You're about to kill yourself. In a few minutes, no one's going to give a damn about you anymore. You'll be gone, and we'll still be here. It's not for you to understand. Are you beginning to see my logic?"

"Not exactly."

"How are you going to do it? Side of the head? In the mouth? Through the chest?"

"In the mouth."

"Good," he said. "That's best. Side of the head, there's too much chance you'll turn yourself into a vegetable. Through the chest, you're not guaranteed to hit the heart. You might only wound yourself, pass out, and wind up in the hospital."

"I don't need your advice," I said. "I want help."

"Help? You want help? What do you think I'm giving you?"

"Not that kind of help."

"I didn't specify what kind of help in my ad, now, did I?"

"No, but—"

"Everyone always *assumes* I'm here to rescue them. I'm not. You want to kill yourself, that's fine by me. I can't abide suicides who get halfway there and then can't finish the job. Some of them only need a little push to be on their way. So I put the number in the paper. I want them to call me at that moment of crisis, when all they need is a little encouragement."

"You're sick."

"Ho-ho!" he said. "You're the one who's already tried to kill himself once this evening, and you want to do it again. Which one of us do you think is sick?"

"Wait a minute," I said, and began to laugh. "I see what you're doing. I can see right through you. You're smart, you know that? You really take the cake. You're using reverse psychology, just like my mother used to do when I was a kid."

"Oh?" the help line said. "Just how am I doing that?"

"By pretending you want me to go ahead and do it, acting like you get some kind of kick out of other people dying while you hang there on the line. You think all we're doing is feeling sorry for ourselves and looking for someone to hold our hands and tell us it's okay, tell us we're somebody special, tell us there's a brighter day dawning somewhere over the rainbow."

"Stop wasting my time. Are you going to do it or not?"

"See?" I said. "Instead of giving us soothing words, you give us abuse. You try to make us feel even worthless, because you think we're going to react against it and tell ourselves we're really okay. We listen to you and think you're a jerk, but we say to ourselves, 'Hey, why should I listen to this guy?' and before you know it, you've cured us of our mania and set us on our merry way. Isn't that how it goes?"

The voice on the help line gave a rude, audible yawn.

"Hello?" I said. "Are you still there?"

"I've been making a sandwich. You were saying?"

"Never mind what I was saying. I'm onto you, and it won't work. Maybe with some other schlemiel, but not with me, man."

"What won't work?"

"The reverse psychology trick. You've just proved to me what a lousy world it is that we live in. I don't want any part of it. I'm going to clean my gun up and blow my brains out."

"Do you really mean it this time?"

"Of course I mean it!" I shouted. "If you want to hear it for yourself, just stay on the line. It won't take very long."

"You promise? You're not just pulling my leg?"

"I promise. Cross my heart and hope to die."

"That's the spirit! Where do you live?"

"Oh, no," I said. "I'm not telling you. Now you believe me, and you want to send somebody over. Somebody from my precinct, maybe, or an ambulance or some goddamn social worker."

"No," he said in that calm, level voice of his. "No, I want

to come over. I want to see it for myself. Maybe I can even help you do it. That is, if you really want my help—"

"I can take care of it myself, thank you very much."

"I'm not so sure. You sound chicken to me."

"Chicken?" I said. "Why don't you go fuck yourself?"

"What's your name?" he asked, unfazed by my suggestion.

"Tom," I said.

"Tom what?"

"Just Tom, okay? I don't want you reporting me."

"I'm not going to report you. You can trust me, Tom. My name's Ray. I'm your friend, Ray. I'm here to help you."

"Lot of help you've given me so far, pal."

"I have," Ray said. "Only you just don't appreciate it. Now why don't you tell me where you live? I want to come over."

"As long as you promise not to interfere," I said.

"Oh, I won't," Ray said. "I wouldn't dream of it."

I gave him my address. He said he lived only fifteen blocks away and could be there in ten minutes. We hung up.

I laid out some newspaper and started cleaning my gun.

"WHY A NINE-MILLIMETER?" Ray asked from across my kitchen table. He was my age, with an altogether too intense look in his eyes. "Why not a revolver? Revolvers never jam. You never would have had this problem. You never would have had to call me."

"If you must know," I said, carefully reloading seventeen live rounds into the clip, "I really believed the nine-millimeter was the way to go. Right after I joined the academy, the department had just changed regulations to allow us to carry something more powerful than a thirty-eight."

"Thirty-eight Special," Ray beamed. "Standard police issue."

"Yeah, in the old days," I said. "Most of us supported the change, but the old-timers were opposed. They kept nagging at us that semi-autos were unreliable and prone to jamming."

"See?" Ray said. "They knew whereof they spoke!"

"They were so scared of the change, they drummed up other reasons. They thought that we youngsters would lose control and empty our clips into every unlucky punk who crossed our path."

"Did they switch?"

"No. They kept their thirty-eight Specials. Switching would be like ending a love affair. Most of us under forty went for the nine-millimeters, though. We were the ones facing the front-line action. The gangstas were outgunning us, with AK-47s, sometimes. We had to be on as equal a footing as possible."

"Thus the Glock," Ray said admiringly. "It *is* nice, Tom."

"Thanks. My Glock and I have been through a lot together. I had to use it once to stop a sixteen-year-old kid who was armed with a beautiful silvery Colt Double Eagle ten-millimeter."

"Do tell!"

"The kid had just robbed a liquor store. I identified myself and asked him to drop his weapon. He refused to do so. He wanted to go out in a blaze of glory, I guess, and I had little choice but to oblige him."

"Good for you," Ray said with a gleam in his eye.

"Ever since, I wished he could have got a bead on me and

let fly. Anything to make it seem less like an execution. But to do that, he would have had to have had at least a few shells in his gun. Once the kid was down, we examined his Colt, and we found his magazine just as empty as mine was after I'd shot him."

"Oh, too bad!" Ray pouted his lips. "Poor Tom!"

"It only takes a second holding that trigger down to let all those slugs come spewing out. I thought I only let him have a few, but the count we did of his chest came up seventeen."

"Wow!" Ray said. "And you didn't get in any trouble?"

"Of course not," I said. "It was all okay. I'd done what I had to do to protect my fellow officers and the citizenry. My captain, Captain Feliciano, said, 'Good work, son,' and gave me this big slap on the back. 'Don't sweat it,' he said. 'He was asking for it, and you gave it to him. Go home and take a nice long shower. You'll feel fine by tomorrow.'"

"Your captain sounds like my kind of guy," Ray said. "Was he right? Did you feel okay about it the next day?"

"Sure, I felt fine. I mean really fine. I believed what my captain said. I'd done my duty. If the kid's gun had been loaded, I might have gotten a commendation for saving the lives of all those pedestrians standing outside the store to watch all the fireworks. Officer Grant to the rescue. Handshake from the chief. Kudos from the mayor. Champagne all around."

"Tell me about the other times," Ray said huskily.

So I told him about the high-speed pursuit up the FDR Drive, when we managed to bring the driver to a stop, and I stayed by my vehicle to cover my partner while he approached the car, and the driver leapt out brandishing a Rossi 851 .38 Special in blued steel. I had no choice but to bring him down. Captain Feliciano later agreed with my course of action, and everything was okay.

Then there was the out-of-control traffic incident, when a Sikh taxi driver cut off a Jamaican bike messenger at a stop-light, and the messenger retaliated by shattering the driver's side window with his bike lock and beating the driver across the turban with it, and the bloodied driver reached under his seat and pulled out a bright stainless Colt King Cobra .357 Magnum and aimed it at the messenger's head with a shaky trigger finger. I was on the corner and calling for backup when I saw the gun. I pulled out my Glock, identified my-self as a police officer, and told the Sikh to throw down his weapon. I gave him more time than I should have, really, but he kept the gun trained on the messenger. Again, I had no choice. I shot the driver dead and charged the messenger with assault as well as criminal damage to property. We later learned that the driver never understood a word of English, but Captain Feliciano insisted that I'd done the right thing. He even bought me a beer.

"I think this captain of yours has the hots for you," Ray said. "He lets you get away with murder because he wants to get into your pants."

"Feliciano? No. If you knew him, you wouldn't say that."

"Yes, I would," Ray said. "Isn't that reason enough to go through with killing yourself? I mean, doesn't that just dis-gust you? You've killed all these people in the line of duty, and you don't even get any suspensions or reprimands be-cause your captain thinks you're a dish. Believe me. I may never have met him, but I know human nature. You're his little buddy, his one special boy. He goes home at night and dreams of you, Tom."

"I doubt that." I laughed nervously. "Feliciano's married."

"As if that meant anything! Tom, don't be so naive!"

"I left him a suicide note," I said.

"You did?" Ray's dark eyebrows rose. "Can I see it?"

"It's sealed, taped to the bathroom mirror."

Ray got up.

"No!" I said. "I told you, it's sealed."

"So we'll reseal it!" Ray said, heading for the bathroom.

"It's for his eyes only," I said, getting up and going after him. "I don't want you reading it!"

"I bet it's a love letter!" Ray shot ahead of me.

"It is not!"

Ray got to the mirror first and snatched the middle envelope of the three, the one clearly addressed to Captain Feliciano.

"Ha-ha!" Ray said, backing up to stand in the bathtub. "I've got it!" He ripped open the envelope, started reading it, and began to laugh. "Oh, this is great! I love suicide notes!"

"Give it to me!" I said, reaching out for it.

Ray snatched it away and started reading it aloud:

"*'Dear Tony'*—Tony, eh? You two are that buddy-buddy? You don't call him captain? Oh, well, never mind—*'Dear Tony, What you see is the end result of my wasted life. I don't know what ever kept me going this long. I guess it was you. You were always there for me when the going got tough. If it weren't for you, I don't think I would have even lasted this far.'*—Oh, Tom, this is a riot!—*'But it's all catching up with me, Tony. I'm a bad cop, and you know it. I can't walk into any situation without my gun going off and leaving somebody dead. No matter what you say, this isn't the way it's supposed to be. Someone should have taken me off into a room somewhere and punished me.'*— Oh, now you're asking Captain Tony for a spanking! Tom's been a bad boy!—*'I don't deserve to wear this badge. But what else can I do? This was my last chance. If I'm a failure at this, I'll be a failure at everything else. I've failed at life. I've got no choice but to end it. Sorry for being such a screw-up. Don't bother sending flowers to the funeral. Save the money for yourself and Stella. Goodbye forever—Tom.'"*

"Give that to me," I said, finally snatching it away.

"Tom, that is so precious!" Ray said. "Can I have a copy? I could just run this down to the Kinko's around the corner—"

"No. Get away from me."

"Oh, Tom! Don't be like that!"

"I think you're the one who's got the hots for me, Ray," I said, heading back to the kitchen table.

"*'I shall but love thee better after death,'*" Ray said. "That's Elizabeth Barrett Browning, you know."

"I used to own a Browning," I said.

I put the letter back in the envelope, resealed it with cellophane tape, and posted it back up on the bathroom mirror.

"What do the other letters say?"

"More of the same. Don't you dare touch them."

I grabbed Ray's collar and threw him out of the bathroom.

"Hey!" he said.

"In fact, I think you'd better leave."

"Oh, no, Tom. I've got to stay and make sure you follow through with this. You might turn back for all I know. I'd hate to come back here tomorrow and find you're still alive."

"Beat it. Out. Sayonara. Asti Spumante."

I gave him a push toward the front door.

"I knew it," he said. "You're chicken. You don't want me around, because you're too chicken to go through with it. You're not man enough. You don't have what it takes to put that gun in your mouth and blow the back of your head off. You're more of a pansy than I am, Thomas."

"Shut up," I said.

"Pansy, pansy, pansy."

"I said shut up!"

"The minute I'm out that door, you're going to turn around and pout and say, 'Oh, my God! What was I thinking? I can't go through with it! I love life *so* much! Life is *so* good!' And then you're going to put your gun away, lock it up in its box, get it out of your sight, and try to get it out of your mind. You'll go back into your bathroom, rip those suicide notes off the mirror, tear them into confetti, and flush them down the toilet. You'll look at yourself in the mirror and thank your lucky stars that your gun jammed and you're still alive. Only I bet it didn't jam on its own. You fixed it up that way."

"I did not," I protested.

"Did too," Ray said. "It wouldn't be so hard. You knew just what to do to make that bullet lodge there in the chamber. Maybe you did it unconsciously. Whatever, you didn't want to do it. Why not? Because you're weak! You're not a man at all. You're just a fluffy little kitten, playing a fun game with a bright, shiny toy. And when the kitten gets tired of playing, it curls up in its little basket and falls asleep. Beddy-bye. Nighty-night. Sweet dreams, little kitty."

I held Ray by the front of his shirt and gave him a left uppercut to the jaw. He swayed, but I held him up.

"Oh, Tom," he said. "You didn't have to hurt me. But the fact that you did only proves my point. What I'm saying is true. You don't have what it takes to kill yourself. You're pathetic."

I let go of Ray, went back to the kitchen table, and stared at the gun. I picked it up and put the last of the parts in place. I slammed the clip firmly into the grip and loaded one more slug directly into the chamber.

"It's all set to go, now," I said.

Rubbing his jaw, Ray came back and sat down across from me.

"You sure you're going to be able to do it?" he asked.

"Sure, I'm sure."

"If you can't quite manage it, you could let me."

"No, thanks. I can do it myself."

"No one would ever know," Ray said. "I could kill you myself, and no one would ever know. Just by putting that gun in my hands and letting me do the job, why, I'd be a murderer. But you've got those notes all neatly prepared — for your landlord, your captain, your mother — and no one would ever suspect a thing. I've got no connection to you. We've never seen each other before. The only person who knows you called me is me, and I won't tell anyone!"

"That won't be necessary. I can take care of myself."

"I'm not so sure," Ray said. "Let's see you do it."

"You better stand back," I said, turning the Glock around toward me, just outside my mouth. "It might get messy."

"I know where to sit to get out of the way," Ray said. "I've done this dozens of times."

"You've what?"

"You don't believe me? You think you're the only special

person in the universe? That's not the first time I've run that ad, you know. You're a cop, you're probably aware of how many people commit suicide in this city every year. A lot of them call for help. Some call me. I try to talk them through it over the phone, but every once in a while I get a really special case — like you — and no matter what time of day or night it is, I drop what I'm doing and come over to see how I can help. I was asleep when you called tonight, did you know that? Yet I hopped out of bed and came on over. How's that for dedication?"

"Then it's not really a twenty-four-hour help line, is it? When you're over here helping me, you're not taking calls."

"I can only help one person at a time, you know."

I had the muzzle almost to my mouth, but I was curious:

"How many suicides have you witnessed, exactly?"

"I've lost count. Funny, isn't it? You'd think that a guy like me would keep a log or something to keep track, but I don't bother with it. Each customer deserves my undivided attention. I don't want them ending up just another statistic. I don't always just witness, you know. Sometimes I assist. It's perfectly legal, you know."

"Bull."

"Assisted suicide? Of course it is! Dr. Kevorkian paved the way. I bet he's lost count of all his assisted suicides."

"There's a difference," I said. "You're not a doctor, and you're not helping people who are terminally ill."

"Don't pick nits with me, Tom! Dr. Kevorkian helps people who are in great pain and want out. I'm no different. Everyone who calls me is in *excruciating* pain. Aren't you? I mean, Tom, the kind of sickness you have, it just eats at your heart, doesn't it? It's painful, and you can hardly *bear* it."

"Something like that," I said, "but—"

"But nothing, Tom! Assisted suicide is the wave of the future. The precedents are set. Soon enough, you're going to see suicide centers spring up all over the country. A whole chain of centers. Suicide superstores, next to every Barnes and Noble."

"You're insane," I said.

"If you're tired of listening to me, why don't you just pull that trigger and get it over with?"

I put the four extending inches of the barrel in my mouth, with my bottom lip resting against the trigger guard. I had it in both hands, with my thumb wrapping around the trigger. There was no chance it would jam this time. It was ready to go.

Ray looked at me with those intense eyes of his. He looked about ready to start slobbering. In fact, he looked lustful.

I shall but love thee better after death . . .

I took the gun out of my mouth.

"Wait a minute," I said, turning the gun on Ray.

Ray's lascivious grin collapsed into a thin red line.

"What's the matter, Tom? I was so proud of you. I thought you were going to make good on your promises."

"Shut up," I said. "I could kill you right now."

"You won't," Ray said confidently. "Everyone else you've killed was armed. I'm helpless, and harmless. You won't do it."

"You want to make a bet?"

"Hey, Tom, come on, buddy! Don't you see it worked?"

"What worked?"

"You were right! I was playing reverse psychology on you all along, and it worked. Another life saved. Damn, I'm good!"

"I don't believe you," I said.

"Don't, then." Ray shrugged.

"You're sick. Death turns you on. Everything about death. It gets you going. Ever since you came over here, you've had this covetous look in your eye—"

"Covetous?" Ray played the innocent. "Covetous of what?"

"Of my body, that's what!"

"Nonsense!" Ray said.

"And you know what? I don't think you're even a pansy or anything. All you care is that it's a body, and that it's dead."

"Tom, I can't believe you're saying that. It's too awful!"

"It's awful because it's true. You don't care how they do it, or why, just so long as you're alone with them afterwards."

"Tom, don't be ridiculous! I do nothing of the sort!"

"Oh, yeah? I don't believe you. And I don't believe you have it in you to kill anybody yourself. In this city, you could pick up just about any stranger you saw on the street, if you were clever enough. All you'd have to do is take them home, or to a dark, secluded spot—maybe the park. If you were capable of killing anyone, that's what you'd do."

"Put the gun down, Tom. You're talking crazy! I'm—I'm worried about you. You don't really want to hurt me, do you?"

"Oh, yes, I want to hurt you, Ray. You bet I do. You're scum. You're worse than scum. You're a scavenger. I'd rather hurt you, but I'm going to take you in. Come on, get up."

I stood up and waved the gun at him. Ray got up.

"Take me in? On what charge? You can't prove any-thing!"

Ray had a point. I had no evidence of his crimes.

"What am I going to do with you, then?" I asked aloud.

"Why don't you just kill me?" Ray suggested.

"No good," I said. "I'd never beat the rap."

"Kill me, then kill yourself. Solves all your problems."

"You have a death wish or something? I'm sorely tempted."

"If that doesn't grab you, why not join me?"

"Join you?" I was incredulous.

"Sure, we'd make a great team! Tom and Ray, the help line boys! Two is better than one. Hey, we could use the good cop, bad cop routine on them! I bet we'd have more successes that way. It's clear to me from that suicide note that you're finished with police work. Well, now Ray's here to hand you back your future on a silver platter. You could quit your job at the police force and come work with me full time. What do you say?"

"You do this full time? How do you make a living?"

"Tom, I thought you were brighter than that! I invite myself in, I help them out, I get my kicks, and then I go rooting around for loot. They can't take it with them, and I may as well have it. That's how I collect my fee."

"Your fee," I repeated.

"You think I'd do any of this out of the goodness of my heart? It's a business, Tommy baby. So are you in or out?"

"How much do you make?"

"Some nights are better than others. I bet you don't have much dough lying around. Maybe you got some baseball cards—"

"You're not getting my baseball cards," I said. "Or me."

"And I was so close."

"Your apartment must be filled with stolen goods," I said.

"It's not easy to fence everything so fast."

"Uh-huh," I said, grinning. "That's what I figured."

I emptied my clip into Ray. He fell down all bloody.

I SET MY GLOCK DOWN on the kitchen table. I opened my front door, looked up and down the hallway to make sure no one was watching, and went into the hall. I closed my door. I kicked it hard three times with the heel of my boot until I busted the lock and splintered the jamb and the door flew wide open. I went to the bathroom, tore down the suicide notes, and set them aflame using one match. I let them burn in my fingers until I dropped them into the toilet, and I flushed the ashes down and away.

I went to the phone and called the precinct house. Captain Feliciano happened to be the operations officer on duty tonight.

"Tony, it's Tom," I said.

"Hey, Tom!" he said. "You're off tonight, aren't you?"

"Yeah, and I had a bit of a problem here. I was just sitting here watching television in the dark, and some guy broke in through my front door. It looked like he was pointing a gun at me through the pocket of his jacket. He said if I didn't give him all my money, he was going to kill me. I didn't want to take any chances, so—"

Feliciano sighed. "How many times did you shoot him, Tom?"

"That damned trigger jammed on me again, Tony, so I blew the one in the chamber and all seventeen in the clip."

"Eighteen, huh? So I take it he's dead."

I glanced at Ray, not moving. "You take it correctly, sir."

"What kind of a gun did he have on him?"

"It wasn't a gun at all. It must have been his fingers."

"Well, that's okay," my captain said. "Just swear in court that you saw the butt of the gun poking out of his jacket. And you're sure he intended to burglarize you?"

"Oh, I'm positive," I said. "He had his moves down cold, like he's done this dozens of times before. I bet he's got tons of stolen goods at his place. Can we get a warrant?"

"Don't sweat it, Tom. You did the right thing. I'll have dispatch send a car over to take your report. Just relax. You don't have a thing to worry about. I'll see to it myself."

"Thanks, Tony, captain, sir," I said, to cover the bases.

Captain Feliciano laughed good-naturedly and hung up.

Ray lay there darkly staining my carpet.

I looked over at my Glock and smiled. In the end, it hadn't let me down at all. It had given me one last chance to prove I was worthy. I picked it up and found the barrel still warm and smoking. I cooled it off with a nice, long, sloppy kiss.

A Doll's Tale

———

I USED TO GET ANGRY whenever Cindy's mommie came home from the supermarket with yet another "demon doll" horror novel. But that was a long time ago, when I was newer, when my dress was clean and Cindy kept my hair brushed, when she spent more time playing with me than with any of the others.

It all started about a year ago, one day when Cindy was sitting on the couch in the family room, burping me over her shoulder. I was looking out the picture window, waiting for her to finish.

Cindy patted me on the back and pretended I was through burping. "There, there," she said, in that high-pitched, squeaky voice of hers. "That's a good baby. Does Huggums feel better?"

She pulled my string. "Mommie," I said flatly as my string retracted. But even at that time I already knew she wasn't really my mommie; I had read the brand on the bottom of my foot: MADE IN TAIWAN. I was nobody's fool.

"Whad'ja get, Mommie," asked Cindy. She dropped me on the table and I lay there on my back, no longer able to see because my eyes had closed.

"I didn't get any candy, if that's what you're looking for."

Apparently because there was no candy to be eaten, Cindy picked me back up and held me upright under her arm. My eyelids popped open, and since Cindy was standing on a chair, I could see the whole table and kitchen before me. Cindy's big brother Rob was there, and I felt embarrassed because my dress had slid up over my waist. I caught him staring at me lasciviously in his OZZY OSBOURNE T-shirt, and quickly averted my gaze.

But what I saw next was even worse. There, among the groceries strewn about the table, was a new horror novel. In red, bleeding, raised lettering, the title was *Die, Dolly, Die!* The cover was black, with a painting of a doll's baby face with green, glowing eyes and fangs protruding over its chubby little lips. I stared at the book in shock, my eyes stuck open.

As the groceries got shuffled around, the book fell on its face. Although I tried to resist, I couldn't help myself, and I read the copy on the back cover:

> *In the terrifying tradition of* The Playpen *comes a novel of unstoppable, heart-wrenching horror:* Die, Dolly, Die!
>
> *Todd and Samantha Morgan had the perfect family and a beautiful house in the quiet town of Badger Prairie. Their pride and joy was their youngest daughter, Tammy, who was "gifted," bright, intelligent, and*

pretty. The Morgans had not a single worry in the world. . . . Until they bought Tammy an antique porcelain doll named Lucy.

Tammy said that Lucy "told" her things in the night . . . that she "made" her do things. And when the Morgans' neighbors started to die, and the school children who teased and taunted Tammy started to die, they realized they were next. . . .

Because Lucy was short for Lucifer, and there was no way to stop her. . . .

Die, Dolly, Die!

I was mortified! How could anyone write something so horrible about a harmless doll? And how could people like Cindy's mommie pay *money* for it and *read* it?

But I didn't let it get to me. I figured I could forgive Cindy's mommie this once. As far as I could tell, she harbored no particular hatred toward dolls, so I assumed her interest in the book fell into the category of "guilty pleasures."

But in the months that ensued, I managed to catch glimpses of other books she had bought: *Witch Doll*, *Baby Satan*, and *The Dolly Upstairs*, to name a few. I began to wonder if there were more to this than met the eye.

During this time, I was treated well. Cindy burped me, fed me, changed me, and dressed me up nearly every day. Often she would invite me to tea parties and jungle safaris with the stuffed animals, and I always got to sleep with her at night, too. Life was easy.

That is, until the beast moved in.

Cindy's parents gave her big brother a dog for Christmas. Not a puppy, but a large, energetic, curious, hungry *dog*. I was in Cindy's closet with the other toys while Christmas was going on in the living room, but I could hear Rob playing with the beast, Cindy's mommie giving him a lecture on its care and feeding, and Cindy saying, "What's his name? What's his name?"

"Ozzy," said Rob.

A little while later, when the family was eating breakfast, I heard Ozzy making his way down the hall. The door to Cindy's room was open, and he lumbered right in, a fat, full-grown, fluffy collie with a tongue a mile long and razor-sharp teeth. Even if I could have moved of my own volition, I wouldn't have; I was petrified. Ozzy sniffed the red shag carpet of the room and then headed for the trashcan next to Cindy's dresser. He buried his head in the can, and when he pulled it out he had the wrapper to an ice-cream sandwich in his mouth.

Within seconds, he chewed it and swallowed it, and licked his jowls. He seemed hungry for more, and continued his search, sniffing every inch of the room.

Somebody call the doggie, please, I thought.

I could hear, from the dining room, dishes clinking and kids talking with food in their mouths—breakfast was far from over. Nor was it over for Ozzy. Shortly, his long nose appeared in the closet, then his whole hairy head and ruff. He cocked his head and stared at me with his dark, water eyes, perhaps sensing my complete state of panic.

He bent down his head and clamped his jaws on my delicate, pink plastic body, and strutted out of the closet. He shook me violently— as if I were some dirty dust rag he could just throw around.

With each swift shake, my eyes opened and closed rapidly.

I became dizzy and disoriented. The next thing I knew, Ozzy was prancing down the hall with me in his mouth, slobbering and panting as he approached the breakfast table.

"Oh!" Cindy's mommie gasped. Then she laughed, and quickly tried to suppress it, probably for Cindy's sake, not mine. *I knew it*, I thought, *she's a doll-hater*.

But Rob and Cindy's daddie didn't care what anyone thought. They laughed away, unashamed. "Get her, Ozzy!" Rob yelled excitedly.

"Hey, Mom, can Huggums be his new toy?"

"No!" Cindy screamed. "No, Mommie, no!" Nestled in her lap was one of those soft, cute, fat, expensive dolls with puckered faces.

"But you don't need Huggums anymore," Rob said. "You just got that nice new doll, and Ozzy doesn't have anything to play with. Or maybe you want to keep Huggums and let Ozzy have your new one, huh?"

"No!" she screamed again, much louder, and began to cry.

"Mommie, tell him Ozzy can't have Huggums *or* Krystle!"

Cindy was hanging tightly onto Krystle, acting as if the world were coming to an end.

"I don't see anything wrong with Rob's idea," said Cindy's daddie.

He wanted to see me torn to shreds!

But Cindy's mommie demurred. "No, absolutely not. I simply will not have it. Huggums and Krystle both stay with Cindy, and that's final."

"Hooray!" Cindy cheered, and kissed Krystle's nose.

Ozzy's teeth, meanwhile, were sunk deep in my plastic

flesh. I was so frightened I wet my panties.

Rob got up and said, "Here, Ozzy, give it up." Then he grabbed me by the legs and ripped me from the dog's mouth. Cindy shrieked.

The beast still had my right arm, which he promptly chewed and gulped down before anyone could take it from him.

But that was just the beginning.

On New Year's Eve, Cindy's parents spent the night out of town at a friend's party, leaving Rob in charge of taking care of both the house and his sister. He took care of Cindy by locking her in her room and invited his friends over for a party. All the kids at the party got excessively drunk and stoned, and the police came twice to tell them they were being too loud. Somehow, Rob managed to clean up the house before his parents returned.

But Cindy threatened to tell.

To keep her quiet, Rob took me from her closet and forced her to watch as he threw me in the clothes dryer and turned it on. He left the door open and kept the machine running by holding the door sensor button with his finger. I was hurled to and fro, tumbling head over heels, my head pounding against the metal walls of the revolving barrel. All the while Cindy screamed, tears streaming down her face.

Rob didn't turn off the dryer until she got down on her knees and promised she would never tell their parents about the party.

But did the child learn from this? Of course not. She kept finding ways to get Rob in trouble, and in turn, he kept torturing me to keep her in line.

When Cindy said she was going to tell their parents about

the stack of *Hustler* magazines in his closet, he took a black magic marker and drew a beard on my face and a swastika on the front of my dress. When she was going to tell about the "funny cigarettes" he smoked, he took his lighter and set my hair on fire, partially melting my scalp. When she was going to tell about what he and his girlfriend had been doing one afternoon, he popped out one of my eyeballs with his switchblade and ran over me with his motorcycle.

After that, whenever Cindy pulled my string, something inside of me skipped and I simply said, "Me, me, me, me. . . ."

Cindy didn't love me anymore from that point on. She left me out of all the fun things, keeping me hidden away in the darkest corner of her closet, with the spiders. Krystle, who never spoke to me, was now the center of attention at all the tea parties, and got to lead the jungle safaris. I wasn't even invited to them. In fact, the only reason I was still around had nothing to do with Cindy caring about me; she was just too selfish to let anything go.

Then one day, Cindy and her mommie were cleaning out the closet when her mommie said, "Oh, Cindy! You really ought to let me throw this thing away." She held me up and looked at me with disgust.

"You never play with it anymore, and look at the shape it's in! Tire tracks! How on earth did it ever get this way? You had better not treat Krystle like this."

"Oh, I don't, Mommie. Krystle's nice."

"So can I throw it away or not, dear?"

"Sure, Mommie, you can throw Huggums away."

"Good."

Throw Huggums away? Good? I couldn't believe my little plastic ears. Cindy was going to let her mommie kick me out of her life, just like that? What was to become of me?

I was thrown into the kitchen trash, where I landed head-first in a pile of refried beans. A few hours later, Cindy's daddie carried the trash sack out to the front lawn for pick-up. By then I had resigned myself to my fate. I decided that dolls were all destined to come to tragic ends, and enjoyed a little consolation by thinking Krystle would someday be thrown onto a pile of refried beans as well. I waited, hoping the garbage truck would arrive soon, but knowing it would not come until morning.

Sometime later that evening, I heard Rob and Ozzy on the front lawn. "C'mon, Oz, hurry up!" I could hear Ozzy relieving himself on a nearby bush. Then Rob said, "No, Ozzy, you dunderhead. Get out of the trash."

But it was too late. Ozzy plunged his head in the sack and sniffed around. Suddenly, he grabbed me in his jaws and took me out of the garbage. He pranced toward his master across the moonlit lawn, drooling all over me. I was glad to be saved from the trash, but as Ozzy came closer to Rob, I wondered which would be worse — to be at the mercy of a garbage compactor or of this metal-head.

"What've you got there, boy? Well, look at that! What was sweet little Huggums doing in the trash, huh?" He leered down at me from above, the bright orb of the full moon reflecting in his black eyes.

Ozzy's breathing was quick, his breath hot; he stood still.

"Hand it over, Oz," Rob said sternly.

Ozzy's jaws clenched down tighter.

"I said, hand it over!"

Rob tried to pull me from the dog's mouth, but Ozzy was too strong for him and darted off, through the open front door of the house. He carried me into Cindy's bedroom and set me down on the chair by her bed. (It made me wonder if dogs can actually *think*, like people and dolls.) Ozzy left and went into the living room to wrestle with Rob.

Cindy was sleeping soundly beneath a quilted bedspread, every now and then letting out a little, dainty snore. Krystle, the bitch, was tucked lovingly under the child's arm.

Ozzy's act had been brave and noble, but how far would it get me? The next day, Cindy's mommie would probably throw me away again, for good. There would be little Ozzy could do against *her*.

I sat there for a long time, just thinking. I wondered what I had done to deserve all the misfortunes I had met with. I had been treated unjustly, even *cruelly* by the whole family, except for Ozzy, who had redeemed himself. But what, being a doll, could *I* do about it? It seemed hopeless, and I became very depressed.

Then the whole house became quiet. I heard the wind picking up outside and the feeble tapping of tiny raindrops against the windowpane.

The full moon was lower in the sky than before and now cast a brilliant ray right into my single remaining eye.

It was then I came up with my plan.

I wondered then if I could speak to Cindy without the use of my string, and say what I wanted to say, and get her to do what I wanted her to do.

"Cindy," I said. I repeated it softly, over and over, until she woke.

"Cindy."

Yes, I could do it!

When she saw who was talking to her, she bolted upright

in her bed and clutched her quilt tightly up to her neck, her
eyes wide and staring in horror. She gasped, and just barely
managed to say,

"Huggums?"

"Yes, it's me—Huggums!" I must have looked awful, with
refried beans on my bald head, beard, swastika, tire tracks,
and an arm and eyeball missing. But I knew what to say; I
had watched TV. "So you thought you'd gotten rid of me,
eh?"

She swallowed hard, speechless, terrified.

I tried to make the moonlight reflect in my eye. I wanted to
look as menacing as Rob had seemed to me. I had to be con-
vincing, because my life depended on it. It was either them
or me.

"Cindy, do you know the big knife your mommie has told
you never to touch? Now listen to me very carefully. There's
something I want you to do. . . ."

I proceeded to tell her my plan, in which she would slit
the throats of her parents, and chop her brother up into tiny
pieces, then go after the neighbors just for the hell of it.

She heard me out, stricken dumb. I think I had her in my
power for a few seconds, but then, from under her arm rose
Krystle.

Krystle looked at me and said, "Huggums, darling, that is
so cliché!"

Krystle told Cindy she was just having a very bad dream,
to go back to sleep, and everything would be fine when she
woke up the next morning; Huggums would be gone.

And that's how it turned out. Cindy's mommie discovered
me before the child woke and personally delivered me into
the hands of the greasy garbage collectors.

It was then I realized those "demon doll" horror novels were entirely works of fiction.

Krystle, you'll get yours!

The Penitent

———

"Ever since I was a young girl I've wanted to torture a beautiful young boy." That was Marie's pickup line on me, whispered devilishly in my ear before I had even seen her face—and it worked. It meant she knew about Donald Fearn and Alice Porter. It also meant she had made a snap judgment about me based solely on my appearance. It didn't offend me; she happened to be correct, though I resembled half of the other people who regularly hung out at the Belfry and probably most of them weren't into half of what I was into.

She twisted my multipierced ear painfully as she took the bar stool next to mine. I winced and cried out, "Ow!" and rubbed my ear to soothe it, counted to make sure none of the silver rings had fallen out.

"My name's Marie." Her voice was high and feminine, honey smooth, sincere—not what one would expect from an out-of-nowhere ear-twister. "What's yours?"

"Gary." Looking at her, I had this sudden, intensely pleasureful sensation, as if someone were plunging a long hypo full of adrenaline straight into my aorta. It was not only her beauty that stroked me but her attitude.

Marie was smiling broadly, filterless Camel dangling, her eyelined eyes boring into mine, irises glistening orange in the candle flame from the bar, eyebrows arched like an arch fiend, hair flat black and stringy but falling only as far as her shoulders, unlike mine, which came to the small of my back. She was all in black from her clinging sleeveless shirt to her narrow jeans to her boots. Her wide leather belt was shiny with sharp chromium studs that would be painful to anyone on the receiving end. She wore only three earrings but many bracelets and necklaces, black rosary beads, filigreed silver crucifixes inlaid with obsidian. The tattoo on her shoulder arrested my eyes: a Madonna and child, colorful and Rapha-elesque, exquisitely inked.

While I was so distracted, Marie yanked me forward by my nose ring and planted one of her cigarettes in my mouth and lit it up for me, then shoved me back to an upright posi-tion, smiling playfully.

"Gary," she said, and coyly blew smoke in my face. "You know I'm not joking, what I said."

"Wasn't that Donald Fearn's statement?" I said. "After they caught him. Only you switched the genders around."

"You know what happened to Alice Porter, then."

"Of course," I said. "I know all about it."

We found that we had a mutual interest in the case—not so surprising when you consider that it was not only sensational and semi-famous but local. We also shared the same taste in true-crime paperbacks and Anne Rice novels and bloody horror movies and punkish-metal, death-obsessed music. We both had come to the Belfry, which some wise saint had constructed in an old Gothic stone church in a depressed and dangerous part of the city. The club draws a batty crowd and has managed to remain minatory enough to scare away the Army dudes, college frat rats, sorority mice, and other vermin.

I asked Marie why she had tried that line on me.

"Because you looked like a likely victim."

I admitted that I was.

"And I wanted to get to you before someone else did."

"EVER SINCE I WAS A YOUNG BOY I've wanted to torture a beautiful young girl." That was what he said, Donald Fearn, back in 1942, before he was sent on to the gas chamber in the state penitentiary up at Canon City. What he had done to seventeen-year-old Alice Porter beggars description — but only a sadist would see fit to do so. All I'll say is that awls, nails, and wire whips were among the tools the deputies recovered from the bloody crime scene, along with the charred pile that was Alice's clothing, and when they hauled the girl's body out of the old dry well . . . well, as they say, that is a deep subject.

I grew up in Pueblo, about fifty miles from where Alice Porter's murder took place and about forty miles from where Donald Fearn was gassed by the people of Colorado more than fifty years ago. My grandpa worked in the steel mill here that covers our rooftops with soot and lends our air its ocher tint and rotten-egg smell — and happened to have produced the sturdy nails that were found among Donald Fearn's "torture kit."

Before his death Gramps would often indulge my pathological curiosity by saying, "Gary, I ever tell you about that candy striper that was murdered up at that old Penitente church back in forty-two?" I would pull up a chair and tell him to go ahead, and we would do some rare transgenerational bonding. Gramps knew such stories would do little Gary no harm. Little Gary was always picked on by the other kids—a wimpy, scrawny, unhealthy-looking waif who never caused any trouble and would never so much as harm the hair on a poor little precious fly. Little Gary's interest in the gory monster movies that came on TV late Friday nights over KWGN out of Denver only showed that he had a healthy, active, normal imagination.

When I was a wee tot, the state DHS deemed my mother unfit to raise me for reasons no one has ever seen fit to tell me. I suspect she was hooked on smack, or else she smacked me around, or else she had a boyfriend who would smack me around on her behalf. The *Father* line on my birth certificate is typed in with a simple X, so either she didn't know who he was or I was an immaculate conception. I'm fairly certain he was not God but probably a Chicano, because I've got that mixed-up look to my complexion, dark coffee-bean eyes, glossy black hair, and I've always taken on a deep, reddish tan when I'm out in the sun for a couple of minutes. Anyway, my grandparents were given the right of ownership, and they were perhaps more tolerant with me than real parents would have been. As they got older, they even put up with my loud, evil music: their hearing was shot. At sixty-nine Gramps had a massive coronary that boosted him up to heaven with the power of a Saturn V rocket. Grandma keeps on ticking, all by herself over in that dirty little old tar-papered bungalow near the steel plant. I visit only when I want to borrow her car.

I can't say exactly how it is that I ended up who I am. Even if I suffered abuse at the hands of my mother or her boyfriend, that's no reason for me to be necessarily drawn to pain. In kindergarten the girls liked to knock me over on the playground, each grab a limb, and carry me around like a jungle captive, but I don't think that's why I enjoy submitting to the power of a woman. When I was a little older, the other boys used me as their victim when we played *Star Trek*, with me getting caught and tied up in all sorts of creative ways, but I doubt if that has anything to do with my interest in ropes and chains. As I grew old enough to enter the shady world of the adult bookstore without being carded, I would scan the varieties of girlie magazines and dildos on the walls, but my eyes were always drawn to the fetish mags, and only those in which the women had enslaved the men. No one ever taught me to find this appealing; it was the same natural instinct that draws the duck to water, the bat to the cave, the moth to the flame.

Most people's tastes are predispositions, things bred in the bone, biological hardwiring, genetic programming as inescapable as Fate. Certain things are scheduled to go off at certain times and you can't buck it, you have to give in. If you try to resist your genes, you're going to short out your circuit board and go careening over the edge, which I supposed is what must have happened to Donald Fearn.

"EVER SINCE I WAS A YOUNG BOY, I've wanted to be tortured by a beautiful young girl." There it was. It was out. I'd said it. Marie had asked me to do my own twist on Donald Fearn's confession, to modify it any way I chose, and to "be honest about yourself." But she had known all along who she was dealing with. She had smelled my quivering sweat from a mile away, across the crowded church floor, through the smoke and haze. She had found the hand that fit her black glove.

"Where else are you pierced, Gary?" she screamed over the music, which sounded like Grandma's washing machine amplified to the nth. The faces hovering around us were ghostly, cadaverous, pale makeup and bloodshot raccoon eyes.

"That's all." What I had were the eight rings in the left ear, ten in the right, and the one in the nose—not one of those dainty things through the side of a nostril, but a heavy silver door knocker hanging down in the middle like on the snout of a Spanish *el toro*.

Marie hooked her forefinger up through it again, and I found myself staring at her sharp, black-lacquered nail as it danced in the flickering light. "I love this one," she said, tugging not so gently. "You mean to tell me you don't have one here?" Her other nails grasped my left nipple. "Or here?" she pinched the right. "Or here?" She tweaked my navel. "Or here?" She grabbed the bulge in my jeans, found the head of my cock, squeezed it. "Nothing?"

"No," I said. Someone had returned with the hypo and stuck the needle straight into my heart muscle. I'd been considering getting other piercings, but I had no one to share those parts of my body with, so I hadn't seen the point in forking over the cash. Body piercing can be expensive, and I was living on my meager unemployment checks after having been laid off from my meat-butchering job at the King Soopers five months ago. My first ear piercing was done in high school, free, by a girl named Snookie with a needle and a cork. I had my later earholes done with a gun at Spencer Gifts down at the mall, which is fairly cheap, and I did my nose myself one night when I was dead drunk on pepper vodka. If left to my own devices, I might have done the rest of myself myself, but on the night Marie grabbed me, I had not.

"I don't feel any others," Marie said. "Show me." She pulled my shirt up to just under my armpits and ran her nails up my chest. The posers around us stopped their conversation and turned to see. "Little pink titties," she said, grabbing and stretching them as if they were Silly Putty.

I winced. Marie smiled and began flicking my nipples with her sharp nails. My cock was trying to grow, but there was no room left in my jeans. She dragged her claws down my skin, leaving long red abrasions, her pearly teeth glowing wetly. There's no greater turn-on than the beatific grin that spreads across a sadist's face as she's hurting you.

"You mark easily," she said. "I love that." She slapped me smartly across the face, knocking my jaw loose and making me bite my tongue. I tasted blood. My heart skipped a beat. My cock found the room it sought. "A nice red glow," she said. With her sharpest nail, she slashed four quick strokes on my chest as if they were the mark of Zorro:

Her finger was red with my blood. She stuck it in my mouth and had me lick it off. She wiped more drips off my chest and smeared them into my lips. She pulled my shirt back down; it soaked up my blood. She grabbed me by the nose ring and hopped off her bar stool, tugging me down off mine.

"Where are you taking me?" I asked, floating in a strange endorphin delirium. She had given me but a taste of what I most desperately craved, like a pusher offering a minuscule free sample of what he had loads of in his truck. She placed her hand in my crotch and felt my hardness: proof, if she needed it, that I was no pretender.

"I don't want to give these vultures a free show," she whispered in my ear. Her teeth clamped down on my earlobe as if she were ready to bite it off. "I'm taking you back to my place, Gary. You're going to like it there."

I followed along eagerly as she pulled me through the crowd, down the cast-iron circular staircase, out the back door, down the dark-alley shooting gallery where people of indeterminate sex were huddled together in the shadows, passing a rubber hose around to see how snugly it could be tied off on each other's upper arms. She took me to her '74 Ford Maverick, held my wrists behind my back and locked them into a set of Spanish-style handcuffs, had me curl up in the trunk, slapped a strip of duct tape over my mouth, slammed the lid down, *chunk*, and shut me in the heavenly darkness.

THE NIGHT OF THE MURDER, April 22, 1942, Donald Fearn's wife was at the hospital, in labor with their third child. Fearn himself was twenty-three, a railroad mechanic. The only reason we even know about him today is because his battered blue Ford sedan happened to get stuck in the mud on the morning of the twenty-third on his way back from killing Alice Porter. A farmer hauled him out with his tractor, and when the deputies later came around asking if he'd seen anything funny, the farmer was able to give them a precise description of car and driver. Otherwise, the murder would have remained a mystery, and Marie would never have had such a clever thing to say to make me come to attention.

Donald Fearn had never even spoken to Alice Porter until the night he picked her up off a Pueblo street on her way home from her nursing class, in the midst of a drenching thunderstorm. A witness heard her scream and vaguely saw her get into a car with someone, and that was the last anyone other than Fearn saw of her alive. Fearn took her out to an abandoned village and bound her to the altar inside the old *morada,* a church that had been built by a devout Catholic sect of Hispaños known as the Hermanos Penitentes. He spent the entire night torturing her while the storm raged and the lightning flashed outside. When he was done, Alice was not dead, but he could hardly allow her to identify him to police, so he struck her head with a hammer and dumped her body down the well. The rain that had provided him enough cover to snatch her had also created the mud that trapped him like a fly on tack paper and led to his ultimate confession, prosecution, and eventual and everlasting asphyxiation.

IT WAS ON GOOD FRIDAY of this year that Marie and I paid our visit to the ghost village to investigate the scene of the crime, like a macabre Nancy Drew with one half of the Hardy Boys literally in tow (she had taken to dragging me around everywhere with my neck in a padlocked dog collar attached to a short leash). I'd read every one of the Hardy Boys books when I was still prepubescent, but even then I had got an almost sexual kick out of those scenes where the two teens were tied up back to back with handkerchiefs stuffed rudely in their mouths. I always imagined they were me, always envied them their predicament, always imagined much worse things waiting for them than what they ever got. Why had none of the villains ever stripped them, strung them up by their ankles, and taken a good cat-o'nine-tails to their virginal flesh?

We arrived as the sun still lingered over the Sangre de Cristos. The dry earth was sun-warmed even though the snow had only recently melted across the plateau. The wind racing down off the mountains was arctic cold, but we both wore our leather jackets, and the bite on my cheeks felt good. The village was a hodgepodge of leaning wooden shacks and old adobe huts skirted by drifts of cinnamon sand. Sagebrush grew everywhere. Tumbleweeds rolled down the barren streets. There were no old movie theaters or general stores or gas stations; the town had been dead for nearly a century.

"I expect to see Clint Eastwood riding in," I said.

"It'll take more than Clint on a horse to save you," Marie said, and gave a sharp tug. "Come on, Gary."

The *morada* stood on a hill a hundred yards to the east of the village, the old wooden cross askew atop the roof. It had not been built in the style of the old Spanish missions but was low and squat, narrow at front and back and long on the sides, with the exact shape and outsized proportions of a great stone sarcophagus. Only one slit for a window, like a gun port, graced the long side, the hand-textured adobe glowing like fire in the sun's last rays.

Marie led me up the cemetery path, past the many rows of weathered wooden crosses planted in the earth, to the *morada* entrance, a worm-eaten old door of solid, adzed timbers.

"This is it," she said. "Where it all happened."

The sunlight fell away, and I glanced over my shoulder to see the village lost in shadow down below, the looming Sangre de Cristos now in silhouette. Donald Fearn had been here. He had known exactly what he was going to do, had probably planned it and fantasized about it for days, weeks. Marie had been looking forward to this night for a long time as well, but she had wanted to wait until Good Friday to do me up right.

The date was significant—nothing to do with Donald Fearn but with the Penitentes, the sacred brotherhood whose secret, bloody rites had taken place within this most special house of worship every year for more than a century before the psycho from Pueblo ever grabbed poor Alice by the hand and pulled her screaming into his Ford and dragged her up to the *morada* and pushed her finally through his looking glass.

BEFORE MEETING MARIE, I'd been staying in a cubbyhole at the Y, and when she told me to move in with her, I obeyed like an old family pet. I had a backpack and an old cardboard suitcase, mostly clothing and jewelry, and a few paperbacks and some cassette tapes, and my Walkman and earphones. Marie had a studio apartment with bunk beds handcrafted out of two-by-fours and plywood, with sturdy hooks and eye screws at strategic locations. She'd had a male roommate who had "vanished," she said, a few months previously—she thought to Seattle but didn't know for sure. He hadn't called, she didn't care. He was a jerk, she said. He had raped her once. She told me to take the top bunk.

She brought me here for that first night of ecstasy, when I had been her captive, her plaything to be bound and unbound at her whim, to be pinched, pin-pricked, mummified, probed, whipped. After I moved in, we spent a great deal of time in the apartment stretching my limits. We seldom had regular sex; usually, when she had bound me or hurt me in a way that satisfied her, she would quietly masturbate.

Our relationship became centered on my transformation. She wanted me to enjoy more piercings and tattoos, and to that end we made periodic visits to the shop run by Federico, a paunchy, handlebar-mustached queer Hispanic leatherman who could do both cleanly and professionally, who had done Marie's masterful Madonna and Child. We could not afford to do everything at once, and we had to wait for me to heal before making each further major alteration. Federico made no effort to hide the fact that he enjoyed illustrating my hide and poking holes through my nether parts, and Marie got off on watching him work.

The process took months, but by the time we went to visit the *morada*, I had rings along my eyebrows, three studs through the tip of my tongue, two hefty rings in my nipples linked by a short chain, rings through my navel, and a whole series starting from my anus, across my tender frenum, along the ridge of my scrotum, up the shaft of my cock, and ending at the head with a massive, weighty Prince Albert of which I was proudest of all and which kept me in a permanent state of semi-erection. Though Marie let me keep the hair on my head, since she liked it for hair bondage, she routinely shaved my body baby smooth with a straight razor, which helped uncover my new tattoos: a green two-headed snake slithering out of my sphincter and onto my left glute, a dragon wrapping itself around one arm, an Egyptian scarab on my other bicep, eternal flames burning at my pubes.

My other tattoos were symbols Marie had appropriated

from the Hermanos Penitentes. Crossing my left nipple:

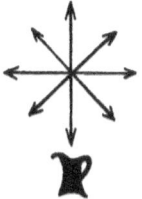

Double-headed arrows in a St. Andrew's Cross superimposed over the cross of the crucifixion, the arrows symbolizing the authority of God, the cup to catch and preserve the blood of the Cristo. My right nipple was crossed similarly:

The cross and four nails of the crucifixion. In the center of my chest, where Marie had slashed her temporary M, she had Federico etch the most elaborate of Penitente marks:

The cross represents the brother hood itself, with the mallet used on the Cristo, the spiked whip that scourged His back, the nails that skewered His limbs, and the cross of thorns with which He was crowned. On my back Marie had Federico tattoo the cross upon which St. Andrew died a martyr:

Once worn by many of the Penitente men, it symbolized those brothers who were prepared to make no less of a sacrifice in the name of the Cristo.

On our last trip, when the last of the tattoos was finished, Marie thanked Federico for all his hard work. He said it had been his pleasure. As he was applying the gauze bandage to the fresh wounds he had carved into my skin, he turned and said to Marie, "*Ecce homo*, eh?"

Marie sized me up from head to toe and smiled at the sight of what she had wrought.

IT TOOK BOTH OF US TO MUSCLE the door open. It was twilight, and the light within the *morada* was blue and dim and fading fast. Marie turned on her flashlight and waved the narrow beam around the barren chapel. The interior was strewn with crushed beer cans, empty whiskey bottles, spent condoms—we were not the only people to have come here in the last fifty years. The low ceiling was hung with thick cobwebs, and I thought I caught a glimpse of a bat hanging in the corner. The altar at the head of the room was hewn out of the same sturdy timbers as the door. The chamber would

have once been decorated with simple handcrafted icons—
carved figures of the bleeding Cristo, images of the Virgin
and the saints in frames of cheap tin. The Penitentes had been
a poor people.

Marie led me up to the altar. "Look at this." With her
bright beam she pointed out rust-colored stains that might
once have been blood. She touched it, and some of the dusty
flakes came off on the pads of her fingers. She wiped it on her
jeans. "So much for Alice Porter."

My heart beat faster, strenuously. I could no longer find
the tiny window, and realized the sky had gone black.

Marie yanked me forward and kissed me, thrusting her
tongue inside to toy with my heavy studs. She reached up under my shirt and tugged on my nipple chain, slid my leather
jacket over my shoulders and down onto the floor. She turned
her flashlight off, plunging us into a void.

"Gary," she said, "are you ever going to get it?"

She pushed me back onto the altar and stretched me out
spreadeagled. She roped my wrists and ankles with a strong,
itchy hemp. The knots were expert, inescapable, tight enough
to impede my circulation. When we'd first met, she had not
made her knots so tight, but we had both discovered that I
preferred them restrictive. I could feel my veins throbbing.
She secured the ends down below so that I felt as if I were on
a medieval rack. Then she took a pair of sharp Fiskars scissors to my jeans, underwear, and T-shirt, cutting them from
my body, leaving me naked, cold, exposed.

Then she left. "I've got to go get the rest of my kit out of
the car," she said, and took the flashlight with her.

For Marie, part of the thrill was playing mind-fuck, and
I knew from experience that she was going to leave me like

this for much longer than she would need to go down the hill. She would want me to think she was never coming back. But no matter how much I trusted her, how secure I was in the knowledge she would return, I couldn't help but panic.

I tried the ropes, but I had no room to move, no leverage, no strength that would amount to anything. The wind whistled through the *morada* and made the door creak. I heard a small animal scrabble in the corner. I could picture Marie sitting in the shelter of her car, thinking about me, thrusting fingers in her vagina, laughing maniacally.

Finally I heard her car door slam shut. But she was not coming back up the hill. She started up her engine, let it warm up for a few minutes, and then drove off. The sound of her car died out a few minutes later.

I was alone. No one but Marie knew where I was. I thought of the Spaniard in Poe's "Pit and the Pendulum," the prisoner of the Inquisition, bound on a cold slab in the darkness, awaiting the giant cutting blade as it swished through the air over his belly, gradually descending, driving him further into madness as the rats gathered below in the pit, waiting for the entrails to come.

The fantasy grew stronger, and I imagined Marie standing over me in a gray cowl, her hand on the lever controlling the giant apparatus, her eyes widening in ravenous blood lust.

I had a raging erection, but I could not touch it. It flopped on my belly like a beached whale, a drop of precum at the tip, the silver rings along the shaft clinking dully and echoing off the walls.

"Marie," I whispered, and smiled. I knew she was not done with me. I closed my eyes and fell asleep.

*   *   *

"WHAT I LOVE ABOUT THE CHURCH is the pageantry and ritual," Marie had told me once at the apartment. My grandparents had been Baptists, and they had stopped forcing me to go to church after my immersion, and I'd never given any religion much thought after that, until I met Marie, who had come to believe in her own personal brand of Christianity. I had come to believe in Marie.

"I'm sure it's not what it was in the days of the Latin mass," she said. "They're losing members, so they think they have to change, do everything in English, get involved in politics, become more 'relevant' to the daily lives of their parishioners. That's why they're losing members! They've taken out the links to the past, removed themselves from the eternal mysteries that held it together. That's why I was drawn to the Penitentes."

"You and Donald Fearn," I said.

"But he got it all wrong," she said. "He may have heard vague stories about them or read the hysterical writings of Protestant missionaries who attacked the rites of the Penitentes only as an excuse to rail against popery. Donald Fearn thought they practiced ritual torture on each other and human sacrifice on the order of the Aztecs—unfortunately for Alice Porter. He was ignorant of their heritage."

Marie told me their rituals had roots deep in the past, further than the medieval *flagellante,* further even than the early, primitive Christians, all the way back to the devotees of the goddess Diana in ancient Hellas, who scourged their own backs in her worship. The Archbishop John B. Lamy of Santa Fe, in the 1850s, tried to brand the Penitentes as heretics and have them excommunicated. But the Church gave in, recognizing them as devout believers, not devil worshipers, though explicit instructions were laid down that they were no longer to crucify any more of their brethren with spikes. By the time settlers came into the West and sneaked a forbidden peek at Penitente ceremonies, they were merely tying their chosen Christ up on the cross, but the blood still flowed down their backs from the sharp bite of their *picadors*.

The Penitentes were simple peasant farmers throughout the Rio Grande Valley and along the Sangre de Cristos, descendants of Spanish settlers in New Mexico dating back to 1598. Their sects had grown only in the rural areas away from the population centers of Santa Fe, Albuquerque, and El Paso—regions where there were too few Franciscan friars to go around. Many of the Franciscans spent more time trying to convert the Pueblo Indians than actually tending to their own flock, and some extorted huge fees for the performance of baptism, matrimony, and burial services. The rule of the Spanish territories became increasingly secular, and with the Mexican Revolution in 1820 all Spanish Franciscans were remanded to Spain—without being replaced. The rural settlements were set adrift with no spiritual guidance until the lands were annexed by the United States during the middle part of the century, by which time the Penitentes were firmly steeped in their own unique tradition.

"The Penitente women were not allowed into their circle," Marie explained. "But after the Last Supper on the morning of Holy Thursday, and all through Good Friday, they sang their *alabados*—rapturous, mournful chants of ecstasy and grief, the Virgin's wailing over the loss of Her Son. They sang outside the *morada* while the men were holed up inside, smoking and praying and selecting the one among them who would become the Cristo. They understood that without the darkness there could be no light, without suffering no rapture. Out of tragedy came not despair but salvation. Out of humility, dignity. Out of penance, redemption. Out of misery, ecstasy. Out of death, life. And glory."

"POOR DONALD FEARN," Marie said, looming over me in the light from the Coleman lantern that stood between my legs. She thrust her awl deep into one of my ear holes, stretching it open with a wrench of pain and a trickle of blood. She removed the awl and inserted a thick pueblo nail into my newly expanded hole. I clenched my teeth and drew in a sharp breath, but I could feel myself growing harder. The pain was everything I had been hoping for.

Marie had returned after perhaps an hour, waking me up with a stinging slap of her palm against my abdominals.

"If Donald Fearn were alive today," she continued, "he might have found some girl who would go along for the ride willingly, without his having to dump her down a well."

This kind of talk was common for Marie when she had me at her mercy. She liked playing the part of the master criminal, telling the hero exactly what she was going to do to him rather than simply killing him in the first place and getting it over with. It upped the ante of the encounter, added a further element of danger and uncertainty.

"Like Jeffrey Dahmer," she said, working the blood-lubricated awl into my nose hole. "He wanted sex slaves, but he went about it all wrong. He tried to do home lobotomies with a power drill, hoping his victims would become zombies who would answer his every beck and call. But they kept dying on him instead. He could never get it right."

She had all my ear holes plugged with nails, and now she

fit a thicker, longer one through my nose. She was turning me into a tribesman of the industrial jungle, plunging nails through every existing hole. The blood was dripping into my nasal cavity and down my throat, and I kept having to swallow it or I would choke. My breathing grew heavy; I tried to control it to keep from passing out. She would continue even if I were to fall into unconsciousness, and I didn't want to miss any of it.

"Dahmer could have gone to those same bars where he got his victims—or placed a personal ad in a magazine—and found any number of willing 'slaves' who'd return week after week and do whatever he wanted as long as he didn't kill them. It just seems like such a waste."

"But he also wanted to eat them," I reminded her.

"Take this, my body," she said. "Drink this, my blood, the blood of a new covenant."

The thick nails went in, replacing the rings at my eyebrows, nipples, navel, frenum, scrotum, and along the length of my penis and at last through the tip of my cock where my glorious Prince Albert had been. My shaft was warm and wet with blood, looking like an erotic pincushion. Every piercing throbbed, my ripped flesh screaming in pain. I made little cries as she worked, tried instinctively to squirm away from her fingers even though this was exactly what I wanted. My body was receiving pain, but my brain told me it was pleasure. Anyone who likes spicy-hot Mexican food has enjoyed a similar response. Bodybuilders grow addicted to their body's own painkilling chemicals after they've ripped their muscles to shreds from heavy lifting. Many people are masochists without even knowing or without admitting it to themselves. Others are sadists without recognizing the fact.

Marie and I were liberated. We knew ourselves. But neither of us knew how far the other was willing to go.

"I don't think I'll ever understand you," she said as she grabbed the heavy, curved upholstery needle and threaded it with a thin strip of rawhide. "You come to me for abuse. That's what this is, really. You want me to tie you up and beat you, knock you around, abuse you. It's what you live for. I'll never see what you get out of it. I cringe if I have a hangnail or a paper cut, but you look at it as if it's some precious gift from God."

"It is," I said.

"Any last requests?"

I looked up at her longingly but had no more to say.

She poked the needle through the corner of my mouth and began sewing my lips shut. When she was done, she tied off the rawhide firmly. She ran her hands along my chest, over my sensitive tattoos, and twisted the nails in my nipples as if she wanted to rip them free.

I tried to scream, but it was horribly muffled.

"See?" Marie said. "Now no one can hear you. I guess we're ready."

She untied my limbs, and I lay there immobile until the circulation returned. The preliminaries were finished. Now was time for the main event. She yanked me by the leash to a sitting position, then off the altar and onto my feet.

"Come, Gary," she said. "Now is your time. You must answer the call of your destiny."

MARIE LED ME OUTSIDE by the light of her lantern. I was naked, tattooed, wounded with nails, the products of my dead grandfather, the tools of the carpenter, the Penitente symbol of the Cristo's suffering. The frenzied wind off the mountains chilled my flesh and made the sagebrush dance in Marie's light. The earth beneath my bare feet still retained the warmth of the sun. More stars were out than I had ever seen, staring down from the heavens, our only witnesses.

I breathed heavily through my nose, swallowing blood. My tongue toyed with the rawhide that sealed my lips. All my senses were heightened, but I was weary, dizzy, my knees weak. Blood trickled down the inside of my thighs, dripped onto the sand. I followed Marie over the hill, my eyes dreamily focused on the lantern as it swayed back and forth like a railman's signal.

We found the well hidden beneath a flimsy square of plywood. Marie knelt down and shoved it aside, shone her lantern down into its depths. "This where she died," she said. "Come take a look. Don't be afraid."

I took tiny steps toward the brink, and Marie encouraged me a little farther. I tried to see the bottom, but the light illuminated only the earthen sides, leaving a gaping blackness. I teetered, felt as if I would fall in, but Marie caught me.

"I've got you, Gary," she said. "I've got you."

MARIE GRABBED SOMETHING from her bag and revealed it to me in the light. It was a *picador*—a many-stranded whip of braided cactus fibers, on the ends of which were attached sharp, jagged chunks of obsidian. She gave it to me, clasped my hands around it. I knew what to do with it.

She walked ahead of me but looked over her shoulder as we made our procession toward the Penitente *calvario*, which stood in the darkness a hundred yards from the *morada*.

I walked as I had seen in the photographs of Penitentes,

hunched over with my back bared to the sky, my long hair dangling down in front, and brought the *picador* down heavily onto my back. Each obsidian rock was a small razor drawing blood. Marie grinned gleefully back at me. I did it again and again, over alternate shoulders. With each stroke Marie changed an "Our Father" or a "Hail Mary." I showed myself no mercy, one flagellation for each step I took, perhaps as many as a hundred until we reached the cross.

My back was a river of blood. The Penitentes had not gone completely naked but had worn white cotton breeches to catch the red flow. I had no such garments, so my buttocks and most of my legs were wet. The wind froze me as if I had just taken a shower and walked out into the cold night.

"You are Penitente," Marie said, though a real Penitente would not have had my piercings—that was her own fetish, inspired by Donald Fearn and her own fertile imagination.

I collapsed at Marie's feet, but she hauled me back up to help her lift the cross out of its hole. It was nine or ten feet tall, built of the same sturdy timbers as the door and altar of the *morada*, weathered, silvered, cracked by storms. Someone had already done some digging around it, and I saw a shovel and another bag of equipment lying nearby. At fist I feared Marie had asked some unknown other to join us, but then I realized this was where she must have come while I was asleep, when she wanted me to believe she had deserted me. She grabbed one side and I the other, and together we lifted the massive cross until it toppled over, kicking up a cloud of dust that was scattered by the wind. My limbs were shaking from the cold, pale from the loss of blood, sapped of strength, soon to fail me altogether.

"You are the Chosen One," she told me, fixing me with

her gaze. "The Cristo reborn. It is your destiny to atone for the sins of men."

A voice in the back of my mind noted that she had not said man or mankind but *men*. But that warning voice was lost in a cloudy haze, of no help to me now. I was so stepped in blood thee was no turning back.

She laid me out on the cross. The cold, gritty wood was painful against my back. I stretched my limbs out along the crossbar, breathing through my nose, relaxing, drifting. The stars swirled above me as in a time-lapse photograph.

"I made this out of roses," she said, and placed the crown of thorns on my head. "Look up at me." In one hand she held a large wooden mallet; in the other, four iron railroad spikes. Despite the cold, despite my weak state, my cock was erect. I had no power and no desire to resist.

Marie knelt over me, her face glowing. She set the spikes down and grabbed a heavy leather blindfold from her bag. Her eyes were dark, impenetrable. I wanted to tell her how much I loved her. I wanted to thank her.

"Gary," she said, stroking my cheek. "You have made me so happy." She pressed her lips against my mouth, painfully, and when she came away her chin was dripping with my blood. She gave me a warm good-bye look, put the cold blindfold over my eyes, and buckled it firmly in back of my head.

I felt the first spike rest in the palm of my hand for what seemed an eternity before she struck, driving through flesh, shattering bone, hammering deep into the wood. An otherworldly scream passed through me, unheard by her except as a whimper through my nose. Blood spilled out of the wound, and I blacked out.

*   *   *

I WAS JOLTED BACK TO AWARENESS as the cross fell into its
hole, pulled into place by Marie and some rope. My hands
and feet were bloated, throbbing masses skewered and held
fast. My head lolled to one side, hair damp and billowing in
the wind, cock erect and pointing up toward the heavens.

"Oh, yes," Marie was saying, far down below, her voice
rapturous, lost in herself. "Gary, you are the One! You are
a demigod! The Cristo lives in you, through your suffering
and sacrifice!" She was breathing heavily, moaning. Though
I could not see, I knew she had removed her clothes and was
fingering herself.

My love for her was unbounded.

She screamed and said, "I'm coming, Gary! Oh, this is for
you, my love, I'm coming, coming . . ."

My mind dreamed up the scene, but instead of Marie, it
was the Virgin Herself, Her hands gone up Her robes, Her
eyes closed, mouth open, tongue stroking Her lips in sexual awakening. I was gone from the cradle, grown, the con-
demned man on the cross, looking down on My Mother as
she came, staining the robes with Her juices. My cock ex-
ploded in a wrenching orgasm, shattering my fantasy, reac-
quainting me with the pain. The warm cum dribbled down
my spasming shaft.

Below all was silence. I wondered if Marie was okay. I
heard her gather her clothes from the dust, rise to her feet.
Then up came a great wailing cry, mournful, grief-stricken,
wrenched out of the depths of her throat. I imagined her tearing out her hair like a woman of Hellas.

I wanted to tell her to shed no tears. The cold wind had
numbed me, freezing the blood on my back and along my

legs. I wanted to tell her to be not afraid. I forgave her her trespasses. She knew not what she had done.

Sobbing, she gathered her tools from the base of the cross and tossed them into her bag. Her footsteps went running off down the hill, and her wailing turned to dark laughter that wafted up on the wind. In the distance I heard her engine sputter to life, and then she drove away. I waited, spent, contented, fulfilled, knowing Marie would return. I drifted off into glory.

"WHAT IN THE NAME OF—" said the sheriff's deputy who found me. They cut me down with a chainsaw. I had no power to move or to speak, but I was vaguely aware of my surroundings. He and the other deputies lowered the severed cross gently and unbuckled my blindfold. It was still dark, but the deputies had flashlights and lanterns. One of them used his pocketknife to cut the stitches on my lips. EMS workers jimmied loose the spikes, released me from the cross, put me on a gurney, and took me to the ambulance the deputies had called in from Canon City, where they took me to a hospital.

"Marie," I mumbled. "Marie, Marie . . ."

"Is that who did this to you?" asked the deputy, who was riding along with me, while the EMS guys worked on bandaging my wounds, removing my decorative nails.

I chose not to answer the deputy's question.

I was in and out of the hospital for months and had countless operations on my shattered hands and feet. Grandma took care of me at her home while I healed. I told the deputies and my grandma that I had been kidnapped by some crazy man in the back alley behind the Belfry. I gave them a description but said I had been blindfolded, it had been dark, and I had only a rough idea what he looked like. Outwardly, to them, I agreed whenever they said I had gone through a horrible ordeal. They said I was lucky, but they meant lucky they had stumbled across me, lucky I was alive.

"We always take a peek up at the old *morada* on the night of Good Friday," one of them said. "There's always someone up to no good. I never seen anything like this, myself. The old-timers talk about some strange sex murder happened years back, but I'd be surprised if it was any worse than this."

I knew I was lucky, but I kept it to myself. I'd had a strange, transcendental experience, thanks to Marie. I owed her. I would follow her anywhere, do anything for her—if only I knew where she was. She had disappeared that night at the ghost village, gone off in her Maverick and vanished. Perhaps she had gone to her ex-roommate in Seattle, the one she said had raped her. Maybe she forgave him now.

When I was eventually able to get around on my own, still with the assistance of crutches, I went back to the apartment and found Marie and all our things gone. I later borrowed Grandma's Pinto and went driving back up to see the village again by daylight. I checked the *morada*, but there was no one there. I went up to the well, slid the cover aside, and shined a high-powered flashlight within. I saw the bottom of the well, but Marie wasn't there.

I hobbled up to the dusty cross that now lay on the ground, stained darkly with my blood, and sat down on its severed stump, staring off toward the sun that lingered brightly over the Sangre de Cristos and wondering why Marie, my goddess, had forsaken me.

THE NAKED TOOTH

———

I LAY IN WAIT IN THE DENTIST'S CHAIR, my tongue toying with my stitches where there remained a dull pain from two weeks before.

Jenny the dental assistant had already affixed the little bib around my neck and I had once again espied the faint black mustache on her upper lip with which I had grown so familiar over the years, whenever she would hover over me to clean my teeth or fix up a rubber dam in preparation for the dentist. From a distance she was beautiful, but up close her facial hair destroyed the illusion. My only consolation on this visit was that I would never have to lie there ever again staring at her mustache.

But Jenny was finished and I was waiting for Dr. Hole, which, honest to God, was his name.

Dr. Hole had been my dentist ever since I could remember. I had always liked him. When I was younger, I was frequently lax in my brushing, and it was probably because I didn't mind going to see him. My mother constantly threatened I would have to have another cavity filled if I didn't brush my teeth after every meal and floss before I went to bed. I could never figure out what was the big deal. You get a cavity, you get it fixed; you shouldn't let it keep you from eating candy bars or drinking pop.

At last, Dr. Hole entered the room and extended his hand for me to shake. His arm was muscular and tan. His grip was so strong the handshake was almost painful, but I always preferred handshakes like that to the wimpy kind. Dr. Hole smiled—a brilliant set of white teeth. I had always imagined him spending hours each day flossing merrily in front of his bathroom mirror. He wore a crew-cut which only now was showing signs of gray, although he had to be pushing forty.

"Ricky!" he said with enthusiasm, still shaking my hand. "How you doing today, pardner?" He offered a wink.

I shrugged. "Fine."

"Good, good!" Dr. Hole pulled up a black leather-padded stool. "Let's have a look, see how those holes are closing up."

I leaned back and readily opened my mouth. Dr. Hole had trained me well over the years; I always kept my mouth open at its maximum width while he worked on me, and he never once had to tell me to open wide. He adjusted the overhead light and turned it onto high. Staring into the light, I heard the snap of latex gloves as he pulled them on, and smelled a faint whiff of talcum powder amidst the regular dentist's office smells and his aftershave—Chaps, I think.

"Beautiful," said Dr. Hole, looking inside. My gaze shifted from the light to his face. A few of his rubberized fingers had found their way into my mouth. He inserted his little mirror and checked the stitches behind my molars: two sites upper and one lower. "Excellent, Ricky, you have got one bee-yoo-tiful mouth."

"Ganks," I said. It was, of course, all his work. I was the only kid in my family never to need braces because my teeth were perfectly aligned, but my cavities were invisible thanks to Dr. Hole's mastery of dental cosmetics.

"No trouble with the stitches?"

"Uh-uh," I said with a slight side-to-side shake of my head. Aside from giving my tongue something new to play with, the stitches hadn't bothered me a bit.

"Good. Well, let's take those puppies out, what do you say!"

Dr. Hole grabbed a small pair of scissors and a pair of tweezers from the tray where Jenny had laid them out, then set to work. He made a series of little snips at the back upper left of my mouth, and then slowly began removing the pieces of thread, pulling them one by one with his tweezers. The sensation was odd and ticklish—yet I remained stock still and simply stared at his chiseled face.

"So, buddy, you're moving to Madison, are you?"

"Uh-huh." My voice was muffled by the presence of his fingers.

"Going to school, huh? Great town, Madison, great town. You ever been there? Beautiful, with those lakes and every-thing. I went out the way a couple of years ago for this den-tal conference. Had a ball! You would not believe this bar they've got there. It's four different bars all in the same build-ing. In the basement there's this gay leather bar, you know, motorcycle types and their little blond boys. Then they've got this regular old bar for straights—kind of boring—and also this dyke bar. Boy, you should've seen the dirty looks I got walking in there! Talk about cold! Anyway, upstairs there's this gay disco with all the fancy lights and everything, lasers, great stereo, and all these pretty people. Jesus, Ricky, you would not believe it. You'll have to check it out!"

I lay there wondering Dr. Hole was telling me all this, but then I realized he must have noticed my earrings and assumed I was gay. Which I was—am—but that's not of course why I was wearing—am wearing—earrings in both ears. That's more of a generational thing. Every guy my age has at least one ring in his ear, and *not all* of us are gay.

But as I lay there with Dr. Hole's fingers in my mouth and my stitches being drawn out through my sensitive gums, I found myself wondering exactly what my dentist had been up to, going to all those different gay and lesbian bars while he was supposedly attending a dental conference in Madison, Wisconsin, and I suddenly had an amazing revelation—that the man who had been taking care of my teeth for all my eighteen years, right here in little old Sherman, Wyoming, was nuts over guys, just like me.

I WAS SIX WHEN I HAD MY FIRST CAVITY, and I remember Dr. Hole was brutally honest with me.

"This is going to hurt," he said, wielding a gigantic silver needle in his hand. He pinched my cheek with his other hand and shook it violently, and then suddenly I saw the needle go inside my mouth and felt it poke my cheek, followed by a throbbing pain as the novocaine was injected into me. "You'll feel some pressure now," he said.

It hurt a little, but it was kind of neat, and I always appreciated Dr. Hole's telling me it was going to hurt. Until that time, I don't think any adults, including my parents, had ever been so direct with me.

The rest of the experience, after the needle, was a cakewalk. I didn't feel a thing as Dr. Hole drilled into my tooth, and I was fascinated by the restrictive rubber dam that had been fastened onto my mouth, and the fact that I couldn't get up and leave even if I wanted to. The noise from the drill was scary, but I simply stared at my dentist's face the whole time and remained peaceful, breathing in deeply. I watched the fine tooth dust billow out of my mouth as the drill charged through the enamel, and smelled the special odor that accompanied it, which I was to smell several more times in the future. I was intrigued by the water squirter with the little vacuum the dental assistant manipulated so expertly, now squirting, now sucking. I loved hearing the sound of the *thoomp!* whenever the tip of the vacuum tube made contact with the rubber dam.

When it was all over, Dr. Hole was very proud of me and ruffled my hair and gave me a small rubber Godzilla eraser. But I'll never forget the look on my mom's face once he was all finished and led me out into the waiting room. My mom looked up at me from a plastic-covered issue of *Redbook* and her face was a stricture of pain. I was all smiles, my face half-numb, and my mom looked as if *she* were the one who had had *her* teeth drilled!

"You should be proud of your little Ricky," Dr. Hole told her. "He took it like a man."

EVERYONE, IT SEEMS, HAS A TALE to tell of having their wisdom teeth pulled, just like old folks all have one about where they were and what they were doing the day Kennedy was shot. Over the years, I think these people have polished their stories and embellished them a little to try and out-do their friends. I was a Nixon baby, and I've never been able to figure out what was the big deal about John F. Kennedy's being shot, or why everybody calls him "Jack."

Felicity Thunstone was my boss at the video store, and she had a wisdom tooth horror story to end them all, which she proceeded to tell me one rainy Sunday afternoon when the store was dead, a few days before my own wisdom teeth were scheduled to be extracted at the hands of Dr. Hole.

"All four were impacted," Felicity explained; where wisdom teeth were concerned, everyone was an expert. "The dentist pumped me full of novocaine and laughing gas, and I was feeling pretty good until he stuck this vise-grip in my mouth and started to pull. I fucking swear it was like giving birth. I kept waiting for him to tell me to 'push.'"

"Did it hurt?" I asked.

"Well, they had deadened the pain, but that's not what's so bad. It's the pulling. There's all this pressure, and it just goes on and on and *on!* After a while you just want them to fucking shoot you and put you out of your misery."

"Why didn't they put you under?" I asked. "My mom did it in a hospital, and she slept through the whole thing."

"That's what I should have done," said Felicity, nodding wisely. "This guy spent hours trying to get that first tooth, but it wouldn't budge. Then the novocaine started wearing off, and they had to pump some more into me and wait for *that* to start working. They just left me there alone with all this crap in my mouth. I think they went to fucking get a bite to eat or something. Anyway, this happened for every tooth. I must have spent ten hours in that fucking chair. That's longer than it took for me to have Cody. Then they put me on Tylenol-3 for two weeks, but it couldn't even touch the pain."

After hearing stories like this, I was truly beginning to worry about the impending operation, despite all the great experiences I'd had with Dr. Hole in the past.

BY THE FIFTH GRADE, I'd lost track of all the cavities I'd had, but then most of them had been in baby teeth, so you would never tell from looking at my mouth. But during my first fifth-grade check-up, Dr. Hole discovered a significant cavity in one of my molars that required immediate attention. My mom wanted to schedule another appointment, but Dr. Hole suggested we take care of it now, and I thought it would be best to get it over with, so my mom went back out to the waiting room with her *Psychology Today* and had to wait another hour or so.

This was one of Dr. Hole's best cavity jobs ever. I lay there patiently while he and Jenny went about their work. It was fascinating to me, and I would use my imagination to try and picture in my mind what it must look like from their vantage point. It was always nice of them to lift up a mirror every once in a while to give me a peek at what was going on inside my mouth, with the rubber dam intact and my bad tooth singled out for drilling.

My tongue was always restless and liked to run itself along the underside of the latex in my mouth, though I tried to keep it out of the way of Dr. Hole's fingers. I always wondered what would happen if the drill slipped and went into my tongue or my cheek, but I was never scared of such a thing happening because I knew my dentist was a pro.

By this time I was going through puberty and was already drawn to other guys, although I didn't have any idea what men actually *did* with one another besides jack off, which I had done a couple times with a few of my pals.

But I did know that I was in love with Harrison Ford. I had thrown myself a boner the previous summer while I sat in a darkened movie theater watching *Raiders of the Lost Ark*. When the Nazis tied Indiana Jones to a wooden post during the movie's climax, I had a little climax of my own. I spent several minutes in the restroom after the show, trying to dry up the wet spot on my pants with wads of toilet paper. But I returned to the same theater nineteen more times that summer of 1981, to watch the same movie over and over, while I dreamed up wild erotic fantasies about Harrison Ford.

As I lay staring up at my dentist while he drilled, with his dentist's mini-headlamp on as if he were a coal miner, I noticed that his features were not unlike those of my idol. His cheeks sprouted the same growth of stubble and he had the same kind of sad cowboy face, and I felt completely at ease in his care.

At this time in a guy's life, he can never tell when he might get hard. As I gazed up into my dentist's eyes and the drilling noises grew ever more intense, I suddenly felt my cock getting bigger and there was nothing I could do about it. Since I was growing quite a lot myself those days, the white jeans I was wearing that afternoon were extremely tight around my hips, thighs, and crotch.

Jenny didn't notice because she was so intent on squirting water in my mouth and then sucking it back out. But Dr. Hole would look away from my face while Jenny was performing her duties and momentarily place his rundown drill on my chest, where he had placed several of his other utensils, and I was sure that as he turned away he had seen the now larger bulge in my pants. I was only half-hard at this point, but anyone who looked down there would be able to tell that was happening, all right, and it made me embarrassed. I wanted to fold my hands in my lap and try to cover it up, but that would only attract their attention.

Towards the end of the cavity job, Jenny had to get up at one point to check on another patient, but Dr. Hole continued to drill. Then, all of the sudden he lay his drill down once more on my chest, only the whirring drill-bit was still winding down. I sat there and watched while the tiny point ripped a hole in my shirt and went on down into my flesh before finally stopping.

"Oh, Christ!" shouted Dr. Hole. "I'm sorry, Ricky, are you all right?"

He withdrew the drill, and a small bead of blood welled up from the hole in my shirt.

With the rubber dam still in place, all I could say was, "Uhn-hunn," but I nodded my head up and down to indicate I was fine. I had felt the drill go through my skin, all right, and it hurt but it wasn't any big deal. During all this, my cock had grown fully hard, and I was more worried about the distinct outline in my white jeans than I was about a stupid little cut.

Dr. Hole patched me up with some antiseptic and a Band-Aid before finishing off my cavity, and even managed to get the fresh bloodstain out of my shirt. Before I went out into the waiting room to meet my mom, we agreed to keep the incident with the drill "our little secret," as if we had been doing something dirty—which in retrospect I suppose we were.

* * *

Having your wisdom teeth pulled is a once-in-a-lifetime experience, which is exactly how I decided to look at it; I figured if you're only going to do it once, you might as well enjoy yourself. And really, how much could it hurt?

So I came to the dentist's office armed and ready with my Walkman and a cassette tape I had recorded especially for the occasion: a full ninety-minute compilation of the finest in high-energy dance music from my CD collection. Within the last year, Dr. Hole had taken to providing headphones in his examination rooms like the kind on airplanes, but the music on his channels was pretty lame, and I wasn't about to have my wisdom teeth pulled while listening to Julio Iglesias.

"Is it okay if I listen to this?"

Dr. Hole and his assistants were preparing for the operation, strapping on their green surgical gowns, caps, and masks, and stretching on their latex gloves. The dentist's coal-miner light was strapped around his cap. Even Jenny's mustache was covered up, and all that remained of Dr. Hole's face were his deep luminous eyes.

"What you got there, pardner?" he asked, looking at my Walkman.

"Dance music."

"Sure thing," he said, ruffling my hair as if I were still a kid instead of a soon-to-be college student. "Go right on ahead! Make yourself comfy!"

The X-rays he had taken the week before showed that I only had three wisdom teeth. Where the fourth one went, I'll never know. Dr. Hole only winked at me and said that having three wisdom teeth was "as rare as a three-dollar bill!" I've since learned that it's not as rare as all that, and also what he meant by a three-dollar bill.

So, I got powerful novocaine injections in three spots, two upper and one lower. Dr. Hole still used the same trick as he had when I was a kid, shaking my cheek violently before the needle went in, and telling me, "You're going to feel some pressure now." I didn't care about the pain, just so long as he was honest with me about it. He was never one for sugar coating—but then sugar, he'd always told me, was "your mouth's worst enemy."

After the novocaine they gave me gas, which I had never had before and which I found truly wonderful. By now, I had begun my tape and was listening to "Venus" by Bananarama while I breathed the nitrous oxide deep into my lungs.

Unlike having a cavity filled, a wisdom tooth extraction is not an interactive experience. Dr. Hole's only communications to me were one-way, advising me of what was going to happen next. I simply lay there, passive, readily accepting whatever he chose to do to me. I had little choice. What was I going to do, get up and walk out of the room? It was something that had to be done. My three wisdom teeth had to go, and now was the time; I might as well lie back and enjoy it.

The operation lasted for hours. I stared up into Dr. Hole's eyes and imagined what wondrous work he was doing inside my mouth. Every now and then he spoke to me.

After some intense pulling, he said, "Ricky, that bottom tooth is a real tough customer. I'm going to have to cut it out."

Okay, I thought dreamily, *do whatever you want. I'm all yours.*

He stuck a motorized instrument in my mouth with a little buzz saw on the end, and set to work. Cutting through all that enamel bit by bit was a long process, and with all the no-vocaine and all the nitrous, I simply lost myself in my music, imagining myself upon a crowded dance floor grooving to Rick Astley or Dead or Alive (this *was* a couple years ago!).

Suddenly in my waking dream was Dr. Hole, in jeans and a T-shirt, dancing there with me. His perfect teeth dazzled me with sparkling reflections of the flashing colored lights of the dance club. Our bodies gyrated and the sweat poured down our foreheads as we danced and danced and danced. . . .

Dr. Hole had to perform a similar dissection on one of my upper teeth, cutting it into small pieces so it would come out more easily. I felt constant attention on my wisdom teeth, whether pulling, drilling, or grinding, and then at last he informed me that the third and final tooth could be simply pulled out.

I'd flipped my tape over several times, going through the Pet Shop Boys, Depeche Mode, Ministry, George Michael, and a number of others. My volume was set on high, and I could barely hear what was going on around me, but I knew that at least a few hours had gone by.

Dr. Hole said something to me that I couldn't quite make out, but then, as if reading my mind, he repeated himself more loudly and said, "Ricky, sounds like a great tape you got there!" His eyes twinkled, the cap on his head framed by a halo of light from the overhead lamp hanging just behind.

Then Dr. Hole set about pulling my last remaining wisdom tooth. He clamped a little device around it and I felt a strong tug. He talked me through it every step of the way as the pressure built. No matter how much novocaine was in my mouth, it couldn't take away that feeling—as if my jaw was about to fall off. It seemed very much like giving birth, just as

Felicity had said, and I could see Dr. Hole's arms flexing as he struggled with my tooth.

"The tooth will out!" he said at one point. After hours of serious operation and all the nitrous they had given me, I felt like bursting out laughing, but I managed to suppress it and maintain myself, until finally, without warning, there was a final surge of pain and the pressure was gone.

I turned off my music.

Dr. Hole held up the fancy surgical pliers, which held in their grasp a bloodied chunk of white enamel. Breathing heavily he said, "And that's the tooth," and from behind his mask I could hear the sound of a raspberry, though I failed to understand why. Since that time, I've seen some old re-runs of *Laugh-In* on Nickelodeon, so now I get the joke.

Dr. Hole had always called me a model patient. I never complained, never got scared, never whined or cried. If he kept a list of good boys, I would have been at the top of it.

I prided myself on following his instructions to the letter. When he opened my mouth and stuck in the unexposed X-ray film and asked me to clamp down tightly and hold still, I stayed as rigid as a statue while he set the long black tube of the X-ray gun against my cheek, fled to the next room, and turned on the switch. I always wanted my X-rays to turn out as perfect as possible, and Dr. Hole was never disappointed in the results.

During a routine checkup in ninth grade, he was looking at my crystal-clear X-rays with me in the light of the overhead lamp when he noticed what he described as "a small cavity."

"How small?" I asked, intrigued.

"It's not really much of anything, but we ought to get it

taken care of or it'll just get worse." Dr. Hole was a strong believer in preventive dentistry. "We could do it right now."

"Okay."

"You won't even need any novocaine for this one," he said.

"Are you sure?"

"Positive. See for yourself. It's nowhere near the root. We'll just drill it and fill it and send you on your way."

He showed me the X-ray again, but of course I couldn't see what he saw. To me, all my teeth looked the same.

"Sure," I said. I trusted him implicitly, and if he said it had to be done, it had to be done. By this time, I was going to my dental appointments by myself on my bicycle, so I didn't have my mom to consult with this time around or to dissuade Dr. Hole from going ahead with the procedure.

"I promise it won't hurt very much."

"If you say so."

So Jenny rigged up the rubber dam and we got started without even a drop of novocaine. When the drill whirred to life, I got a little apprehensive, recalling that scene in *Marathon Man* where the old Nazi dentist Laurence Olivier worked on Dustin Hoffman's teeth without any novocaine, as some form of torture. But once the drilling was underway, I realized that was only a silly movie. There was really nothing to it.

"Here, Ricky," said Dr. Hole during a break in the drilling. He took my hand and guided it to his left arm, which was resting at my side. "Hold onto my arm, like this. If it really starts to hurt, just squeeze, and I'll give you some novocaine, okay?"

I nodded, but I had full faith in him. With my hand resting on his hairy muscular arm, I knew I would be all right.

The whirring of the drill grew more high-pitched as the

drilling itself grew more intense, and I began concentrating on the feel of his arm beneath mine. I looked up and saw my own fish-eye reflection in the iris of each of his eyes, and wondered for the first time exactly what he saw when he looked at me.

Back then, I had no inkling that he might be gay. All I did know was the gossip that went around town. He had recently divorced from his wife, and his two kids were among the most screwed-up in the community. His son Brad was fifteen, same age as me, but hadn't been seen around school in some time because he was spending time in a drug rehab clinic. His daughter Gwendolyn had supposedly had a baby when she was sixteen, dropped out of school, and run off with a group of Satanists called the Rainbow Family. Shortly after Gwendolyn ran off, thousands of dollars worth of electronics equipment were stolen from Dr. Hole's home, and there was little doubt as to the culprit. His marriage had been unable to withstand the pressures, everybody said, and thus they had split up. The only hint I might have had that he was gay was the pink BMW he drove, which I had always assumed had been his wife's.

The drilling on my tooth reached the point where I was feeling some pain, but it was endurable. Dr. Hole had promised the cavity was "shallow" and that it wouldn't take long to drill out. I knew it would only be a few more minutes, so I held off on squeezing his arm.

I watched the tooth dust this time wondering when it was going to end. The pain was becoming raw and piercing, but I remained calm and put up with it.

Dr. Hole paused for a moment, withdrawing the drill and letting it wind down before placing it on my chest. He examined the tooth closely and then said, "Hmm, I guess it's deeper than I thought."

I made a sort of moaning sound from behind the dam.

"Well, there's no point in giving you any novocaine now. We're almost finished. Just squeeze my arm if you feel anything."

The drill started up again, whirring and grinding, whining and scraping.

Before a minute was out, I felt a sudden excruciating jolt of pain sear its way from my tooth to the center of my skull.

My hand clutched his arm so tightly that one of my fingernails drew some of his blood.

"There," he said, and the drilling was done. "You okay?"

I nodded, sweating like crazy, my heart palpitating.

"Good. You are such a good sport, Ricky."

When he had filled my tooth and removed the rubber dam, he asked me again how I felt.

"Fine," I said.

"I thought you were going to tear my arm off, pal!"

"No, no, I'm fine."

"Kind of a rush, wasn't it?" he asked, eyes agleam.

"Yeah," I said, unable to hold back a smile. "Yeah, Dr. Hole, it kind of was."

ONCE THE STITCHES WERE all out, Dr. Hole examined his handiwork to see how well the holes had closed up. "Beeyootiful!" he said. "I've never done a better job."

"Hey, I appreciate it," I said, and meant it.

"Well, Ricky, I guess that's just about it. Why don't you follow me?"

He led me out of the examining room and down the hall,

into his office, and closed the door behind us.

"I'm sorry to see you go," he said, sitting behind his desk and bidding me sit before him.

"I doubt I'll find a dentist in Madison as good as you."

"Let me tell you, it's been a treat having you for a patient. You can't imagine how depressing this job can be. Sometimes you feel like everybody hates you. Grown men shrinking from needles, people worried about getting AIDS, children bawling their heads off. It's not easy."

"Guess not."

"I don't have any other patients like you."

"They must have broke the mold," I said, and yes, I was flirting. After all, I'd had a crush on him since I was a kid.

"Have you ever thought of going into dentistry?" he asked. "I think you'd do a fine job."

"No, sir. I'd rather be on the receiving end."

"Oh, please," said Dr. Hole, running his fingers through his bristly crew-cut. "Don't tease me. Come here."

He motioned to his lap.

I came around the side of the desk and sat on his knee as if he were Santa Claus.

"One arm over here," he said, directing my arm around his shoulders. "This one over here." He placed my other hand at his middle, and I could feel that his abdominal muscles were firm.

His smile was magical, and his eyes revealed to me a wisdom never to be found in any tooth.

"I really have to go," I said.

"I know," he said.

"I have to finish packing. I'm leaving tomorrow."

All Dr. Hole did next was to close his eyes and part his lips, and I knew then that this was an invitation. I kissed him full on the lips, and our tongues met. When we broke a moment later, Dr. Hole was smiling broadly, his eyes still closed. He snapped out of his reverie only when I got up from his knee.

"Ricky?" he said, his voice almost pleading.

"I really have to go." I was already halfway across the room.

"Wait," he said. "I've got something for you."

He reached into the lower drawer of his desk, but I couldn't see what he was doing. All I could think of was the rubber Godzilla eraser he had given me after my first cavity, which I had foolishly used up long ago. I would have given anything to have it back.

"Couldn't save the first two," he said, holding up a small glass jar containing a tooth in clear water. "Had to cut them all up. But I . . . I thought you might want this."

I took the jar, held it up to the light, and examined the huge wisdom tooth he had extracted from me two weeks before.

"Thanks," I said, for lack of better words.

He gave me that rough handshake of his, and said, "I'm really going to miss you, pardner."

I looked at his sad exquisite face and handed him back the tooth. "You know, Dr. Hole, maybe you ought to keep this for yourself."

He took it from me with reverence as if it were the Hope Diamond, and set it on his desk next to the two framed photos of his now-grown kids. A tear fell down his cheek and he muttered, "Christ."

I wanted to reach out and help him somehow, but I had done all I could.

"Well, Ricky, I don't want to keep you."

Please do, I thought. *Please keep me.*
But all I said was, "Yeah, I really have to go."

THE CAT'S MEOW

———

1982.

THE CAT'S MEOW DREW ROMAN DEPAUL to an open field on the edge of town. It was a helpless sound—scared, alone. The cat was calling. Hidden, afraid. Roman heard its call and longed to find it; he was lonely himself, it was night, and it was *cold.*

He paused at the curb and peered through the darkness, but couldn't see anything over the mounds of earth in his way. The field was a dumping site for dirt dug from the basements and foundations of houses; it was overpopulated with tall mounds of gray and brown earth stretching far and wide, many taller than Roman himself. The full moon dimly lighted the mounds while thick clouds passed before it, making shadows dance.

The wind grew in strength but the cat's meow was still audible. The cold became colder and Roman's tattered Army jacket was of no use against it. His mouth was dry and without taste; he had gone all day without wine since he hadn't the money to pay for it.

So lonesome. . . . You've led a lousy life, buddy. And where did it get you? So lonely you need a friend tonight or you'll go crazy. And what sort of friend are you going to wind up with? A cat. A friggin' *cat* of all things!

The cat was calling from the mounds, the whining sound echoing through the wind before being lost. Roman listened, pulling his jacket tighter around him.

Meow.

Coming from the mounds, shadows dancing.

Roman took a deep breath and started up the first gray mound. The earth was frozen and rough. Up the mound, then down, suddenly hidden from the street. The next mound was just as tall, and when he reached the summit he was attacked by the swirling wind. Down again, between mounds where the wind wouldn't go, then up. The cat's meow surrounded him at times, but at others it came from one direction. The wind swirled through the shadows.

"Alfred?" Roman whispered.

1934.
"What a stupid name!"

"Roman," scolded his mother. "I think you owe your little brother an apology. After all, it's his cat and he can call it whatever he wants."

Roman glared at Joey, who sat contentedly on the sofa with a kitten in his lap.

Alfred, purring, looked up at Joey's face and grinned.

Roman stomped up to his room. So how come he got a cat, huh? What makes little Joey so deserving? Stupid cat.

He kicked the wall. Hard. Hard enough so that on the other side of the wall, the glass-encased portrait of his grandmother fell to the floor and shattered.

Damn you, Alfred; now you got me in trouble!

1982.

ROMAN SWALLOWED HARD and continued to trudge over the tall piles of unwanted dirt.

Alfred is long gone. He ran away. Watch it or you'll look even older when this night is through. Just find that damned cat.

No one ever talked to Roman. "Crazy Roman," they said. Stay away from Crazy Roman. Just ignore him. Let him climb into his bottle and stew. If you see Crazy Roman in your path, go to the other side of the street; that way you'll be safe. Never know just what he might do. Be good or Crazy Roman will get you!

Roman had always been lonely, it seemed. He *had* to find that cat.

It called again. How many mounds had he climbed over? And how many more would it take? In his old, battered condition he was growing weary.

This is so difficult in this cold. But I'll make it up to you, Joey, just wait and see.

1935.

IT WAS COLD THAT MORNING, and Roman's mother served cold cereal. He would have preferred a hot breakfast, but his mother was in a crabby mood and he said nothing.

After a bad day at school, Roman sat by the fireplace in his living room with his pile of books and list of assignments. Alfred crept over to him and rubbed against his leg. "Go away, you stupid cat," he shouted. "You're getting hair all over me. Yuck! Go away!"

Alfred gazed into Roman's eyes with a smirk on his face.

"Don't look at me that way, Alfred, I'm no dummy!" He grabbed the cat and in a fit of fury threw it against the wall. "That'll show you!"

Just then Joey walked in a burst into tears as the cat tumbled off the wall and onto the floor, a trickle of blood tracing a line down its chin. "Don't you ever do that again, Roman!" His face was wet and his chest convulsed from the tears.

"Oh, go cry somewhere else, dammit!" Roman said.

"Watch your language, Roman," said his mother from the kitchen.

Damn.

1982.

THE WIND WHIPPED AND SWIRLED. Roman pressed forward, searching for the cat. *Alfred.* Although he was only sixty-two, he was feeling more and more like ninety. *I'll make it up to you, Joey.*

The wind . . .

Over the mounds. *And through the woods —to Grandmother's house—except that Grandma didn't like cats.* More mounds, all of them difficult. At last, reaching the windy top of a gray mound he saw the two green eyes reflecting the moon's glow, peering up from the shadows below. He stepped down the steep slope, excited, happy, but knowing to be careful so the creature wouldn't get scared. The last thing he needed was for that cat to run off after all the work it had taken for him to find it. Roman sat to rest on the floor of a miniature valley with miniature mountains surrounding him—and two green eyes only feet away. A call came from invisible lips beneath the eyes. The creature was hidden by the shadows.

"Here, kitty," said Roman DePaul in his normal voice that made him sound older than he really was. The staring eyes blinked. "Here, kitty."

Not wanting to scare the cat, he tried to be patient.

Meow.

1935.

A month after he had thrown Alfred against the wall, Roman felt better. Spring was taking over; it was gorgeous outside. Roman was having an all-around good day. It was Saturday and there was no school. Mom, Dad, and little Joey had gone into the city to do some shopping. They would be gone all day. And even though Roman had been much nicer to Joey lately, it was good to have the little bugger gone for once.

He was sitting on the weathered swing on the front porch in the warm, humid air, drinking lemonade out of a pitcher. He had made it himself; even though it didn't taste like Mom's lemonade it was still cold and refreshing. The air inside the farmhouse had been getting stale, so Roman had left the front door open wide to air it out. Who cared if a few mosquitoes went in? The air in there had also been smelling of cat.

It was certainly a good day to mess around. No parents, no little brother, just a bunch of trees—bare ones, alas—and a big house and a nice trail up into the hills. . . .

Suddenly, an idea struck him to try out Dad's new motorcycle. It was heavy, but he managed to get it out of the barn and into the open. It was an odd piece of machinery: only a little metal frame connected to two wheels with handlebars to steer the front one, and a small engine lashed somehow onto the frame which made it go by means of a chain. Easy. Dad had explained it to him. It was difficult to remember, but he soon figured out how to start it, and it ran—he was lucky, he guessed. Now one of the these levers on the handlebars was the clutch. He pulled the one on the right and tried to shift into first, but it didn't work, so he pulled the left one. It worked. The saddle on the motorcycle was very different and it took him a moment to get situated on it, but then he let out the clutch—slowly like Dad had said.

And he was off. It wasn't much harder than riding a bicycle, and he sped off into the hills. Soon the farmhouse was too far away to see. The trail went on and on. Eventually Roman realized he would have to turn back.

How much gas was there in the tank? If it ran out of gas, Dad would kill me, 'cause then he'd know I'd been riding it. *Not without my permission . . .* damn. There may not be enough gas.

Finally he rode over a hill and could see the house, surrounded on both sides by thick clumps of bare trees. He had to go through the trees to reach the barn, so he slowed down to a moderate speed and weaved his way through. Then he nearly put the bike away, but he began thinking how fun it had been going through the trees. It had been easy. No challenge at all. Looking over at the back of the farmhouse, Roman decided just to take a quick hop around the house, hitting the sections of trees on both sides, and *then* put the motorcycle back in the barn. He let out the clutch and the handbrake and went off into the trees on his left. He picked up the speed and zipped through with no problem at all—well, one tree had come close. But he knew he could do even better on the other side. He maintained his high speed and dodged the tree trunks carefully as he rode towards the barn.

What a thrill! And with no one around to bother him.

Until suddenly someone was around to bother him. Alfred. He must have escaped the house through the front door. He was lounging in the shade of a tree trunk's long shadow when Roman saw him lying directly in his path.

There would have been time to stop . . . if only he had grabbed the handbrake on the right side of the handlebars instead of the clutch on the left. Roman couldn't have turned to miss the cat because he would have slammed into a tree on either side of it and hurt himself.

He slid the bike to a stop and ran back to the cat. He panicked. Alfred was dead. It was a messy sight. The blood — and the mangled body — and the ghastly face — and the *blood!* It sent Roman running into the bushes where the lemonade came up from his stomach.

Oh God oh God oh God! Alfred! Joey's most favorite thing in the world. And with Dad's motorcycle. Without permission. Big trouble. Big *trouble*. Oh, God. What to do.

Cover it up. Cover it up. Wipe the evidence. Yes, yes. Fill the motorcycle's gas tank, pray the bike's not damaged, bury Alfred, wipe up the blood on both the ground and the tires, and tell everyone that Alfred ran away. With another cat. Do it now, dammit, before they get back!

He frantically went to work covering up the whole stupid mess.

Murder. No, it wasn't murder, not killing a cat, no. Besides, it was an accident. It was just a crummy accident, dammit! Oh . . . damn.

*   *   *

1982.

THE CAT CROUCHED in the shadows. It didn't move, so Roman continued to rest from his over-exertion.

"Do you know a kitty-cat named Alfred?" he asked. The glowing eyes blinked once. Roman chuckled. "I knew a cat named Alfred once, a long time ago. But he was a mean kitty-cat. He always stuck his nose into other people's business where it didn't belong. I didn't like him too much. He didn't like me very much, either, let me tell you. But then one day he ran away with a lady cat named Priscilla and he didn't ever come back. Funny, huh? Never came back, the dumb cluck." He chuckled and saw the cat's staring, glowing eyes. "But," he said with a short chuckle. "But you aren't like Alfred. You're a good kitty-cat. You won't—you won't run away from me and little Joey, will you? I didn't think so. Yeah, you're a good kitty-cat. C'mere."

A paw emerged from the darkness, leading the cat out of the shadows. It was a black cat. So what. It approached slowly, finally reaching Roman and rubbing against his leg. Its coat glistened in the moonlight; it was a beautiful and mysterious animal. Roman had thought from the sound of its cries that it would be thin and sickly, but on the contrary it was plump. There was no collar or name tag on it—a stray. Good.

"How'd you get so fat, cat?" It purred an answer, a familiar smirk on its face. Coming closer, it crept up to rub against Roman's ribs. The creature seemed to take note that the ribs were rising and falling at a fast rate. It meowed once and then purred as it crept, reaching the man's shoulder. It smirked again, looking directly into his eyes.

"Don't look at me that way, Alfred, I'm no dummy!" he snapped. He quickly jerked over to reach for the cat, but stopped himself at the last second. "I'm sorry." A tear rolled down his cheek. "Alfred ran off. But I'll be nice to *you,* cat. Sorry."

The black cat crawled onto his chest and licked his chin. Roman grinned wide, childishly.

Then the cat jumped from his chest to the frozen ground and strutted off to the shadows. From being in the field so long, Roman's eyes had adjusted to the darkness and he could see detail through it. The cat perched itself atop a small, long mound of loose dirt. *Loose,* not frozen. It walked in a tight circle on the mound a few times, then dug a small bit of earth with its hand legs.

Meow?

1935.

THE WORST THING ABOUT IT WAS, Joey believed the story. So did Mom and Dad. At first Roman was relieved, but after a time he thought about it more deeply. With Alfred running away, why didn't Joey cry or something? He must have fallen out of love with it. He didn't even cry. All he did was ask, "Was Priscilla a pretty cat?"

Roman felt worse guilt from then on. Why hadn't he just told them the truth? It was an accident, after all. Joey would have understood.

But as time passed, Joe, Mom, and Dad all forgot about Alfred. Joey received a goldfish named Hank for his birthday. But Roman didn't forget. Alfred the cat haunted his conscience. Some nights he was running to the bathroom to vomit after reliving the sight of Alfred's bloody death over and over again in his nightmares. The bloody tire tracks on his fine fur. The ghastly face. Alfred's body was now hidden in a deep grave no less than five yards from the backside of the barn. and as long as they lived at the farm, Roman prayed no one would find it, rotting unprotected in the earth.

1982.

IN THE SHADOWS. Where Roman could see. The dirt in the long small mound must have been entirely dug by the cat itself. The tracks of its paws were all over the pile, grooved into the loose dirt, here and there.

The cat cried out again, scratching its hind legs in the dirt.

Roman stared, wondering.

It began digging larger amounts of dirt.

"What do you want now?" The cat ignored him and continued digging. Roman sniffed and coughed. "You gotta co-operate with me. I'm going to be nice to you, remember? I'm not going to hurt you, don't worry."

The cat smirked; it wasn't worrying.

"God, you're plump, kitty-cat. Alfred was never as fat as you. That lady cat he ran off with probably fattened him up some. Do you think?"

Meow. Smirk. Digging through the sand frantically.

Roman rose, still tired from the walk, and went to the cat in the loose mound of dirt in the shadows. As he approached, the cat dug quicker and quicker, its glowing eyes glancing up for a moment.

"Here, let me help you," Roman said. "Friends help other friends, you know. And you're my friend. You don't call me Crazy Roman. That's 'cause you have morals, not like those dumb housewives think they know everything in the whole damned world. Stay away from Crazy Roman! Heh-heh."

The creature dug quickly, more furiously. Shadows danced.

1977.

AT JOEY'S FUNERAL ROMAN CRIED. Sure some normal thoughts went through his mind: *Why did he have to go first? Just a freak accident, but it happens. Lightning. Never thought it would get little Joey.*

But the thing that kept sticking in his mind, the thing that outweighed all the others was: Why didn't I ever tell Joey the friggin truth about Alfred? He never knew.

1982.

ROMAN KNELT DOWN AND BEGAN to scoop away cold handfuls of dirt. But suddenly he broke into a loud sob and sat.

"Dammit, cat, it's a lie!" he said. "For—five years I've been *lying* to myself." He sniffed, then broke into a wail, water gushing from his eyes. "Alfred didn't run off with a pretty cat. No, he didn't, honest! I lied to you, too. It—it was all my fault. I killed him. Yes, yes! I killed him. It was an accident, I swear." Sniff. "I—I ran over him with a—with a motorcycle." He cried for a moment, then lifted his hands higher, his face dripping. "Don't ever use it without my permission. That was Dad. He said not to use—use it. But he was gone. I shouldn't have *ever* taken out that damned machine." Sniff. "He just sat there and I—I—I plowed him down, flat as a pancake! Honest!"

The cat kept digging, and Roman joined in, crying.

"You aren't flat, you're a fat cat. What are you looking for, you fat cat?" He chuckled, then sobbed again.

The cat kept digging.

Roman stopped crying and wiped his face dry with the cold palms of his hands. He looked at the cat, so serious in its work. "You *will* forgive me, won't you?" He waited for a response, his hands clasped.

The cat dug deeper.

"Oh, cat, won't you forgive me? Won't you?"

Dig, the cat seemed to say.

So he dug. And he found something in the earth. "Ah-hah!" he said before pulling out the objects. "You will, you *will!*"

But he gasped when he saw what he was holding: bones from a human hand, and the blood and flesh clinging to them. He threw them down, not scared, merely blank.

The cat shook its head slowly from side to side: *No.* With a smirk.

Absently, Roman dug, uncovering further remains. The arm bones, the clavicle, some ribs. A grin started at the corner of his mouth. He found a large chunk of torso, heavily clawed.

Buried in the earth.

(In a deep grave behind the barn, where no one would find it.)

The bloody tracks of ripping claws.

(Bloody tracks of a motorcycle on his shiny fur.)

"Just like Alfred," he muttered, then began to chuckle. He cackled loudly and sat, the cold ground beneath him, the moon far above. The wind swirled and shadows danced. He looked at the cat while he laughed wildly. It was smirking again.

"Did—" His eyes were wet. "Did Alfred send you?"

The black cat shook its head: *No.*

Roman stared for a moment, then laughed hysterically. "Joey! Ha-ha, I'm right! Joey sent you!" His mouth stayed open, agape in a grin, water pouring down his face in streams.

The cat, eyes aglow, nodded its head, purring: *Yes.*

Roman drew his muscles taut, curling into a ball as he rolled and rolled on the frozen ground, laughing too hard to stop. Clouds passed before the moon.

His laughing died down enough for him to sit up and face the cat, though he couldn't help bursting with laughter now and then. "Well, cat. I guess this means you aren't going to forgive me, huh? Or should I say, Joey isn't going to forgive me?"

The cat shook its head slowly, with a smirk.

Roman laughed. "Ha-ha! Would he—would he have forgiven me if I had told him the truth?"

The cat seemed to shrug.

Roman's stomach ached from his hysterics. He rolled in the pile of flesh and bones, wiping the tears from his face. "And I never told him! I never told the truth to the little bastard! Ha-ha!" Roman laughed himself into oblivion.

"And," he said. "And you—you killed whoever-this-is? This pile of bones? Just like I killed Alfred! Didn't you get the wrong guy?" He laughed so hard he nearly died right there.

It was an accident; Joey said you'd understand. The cat purred.

Roman couldn't help but smile. "I'm next, right?"

It nodded: Yes.

"The funniest thing is—I never told Joey the truth! I—I told him—hee-hee—Alfred ran off with a lady cat named—named—*Priscilla!*"

The cat crept closer to Roman, who lay aching in the pile of bones.

Roman barely managed to say anything amid his cackling. "You going to kill me now? *You*, a worthless housecat?"

It shook its head from side to side. *No, not* just *me.*

Roman had wondered, why a cat? Why not a tiger? He didn't need to wonder any longer. Suddenly, there were hundreds of dark shapes and glowing eyes above him, perched atop the surrounding mounds. Joey had sent hundreds of worthless little housecats. This was unbearable to Roman, and he broke into hysterical laughter, rolling around on the ground as the cats crept down the slopes, meowing in unison. It was the meow, the call of helplessness which had drawn him there in the first place.

Roman tried to say something. "Joey sent—" was all he managed to say. The laughter won.

But the cats' meow was not a cry of helplessness, it was a cry of hunger. The cats, hungry for his fleshy; and little Joey, hungry for his soul. From the laughing, the crying, and the pain in his stomach he was helpless.

The cats crept closer.

Meow.

Spoiled Rotten

———

Parker stared at the things in his refrigerator, most of which were no longer food. What had once been macaroni and cheese and sliced franks now looked like something else entirely. The milk was curdled, the cheese was green and fuzzy, the two remaining tortillas were dry, and an entire head of lettuce had turned dark brown, the color of toast. The only thing still any good was an unopened can of beer, but it had been a while since Parker had had the inclination to have beer for lunch.

It couldn't be time to get groceries again, he thought as he shut the refrigerator door. It seemed too soon.

His stomach was grumbling, so he grabbed his wallet, put on his wool jacket, and left the apartment, his eye on fast food, preferably something Mexican. He felt like tacos. His mother would have said, "You don't look like tacos," but then she lived fifteen hundred miles away, thank God. There was a Taco Bueno several blocks down the boulevard, its bright plastic sign partially obscured by the blowing dust.

The West Texas wind seemed to have found new life this morning, as if trying to make the transition from winter to spring as brutal as possible. It picked up dust and weeds as it went and spat it in people's faces, except there were few people out; most of the students were gone for spring break, and everyone else was either out for Sunday dinner with their families, or home spending a lazy afternoon in front of the TV.

Parker couldn't believe it was spring break already, but he hadn't attended classes in a few weeks, so he figured his inner calendar was simply off. He liked staying in town during spring break anyway, because the desolation calmed him.

The wind caught the door as he entered Taco Bueno, but the pneumatic device at the top of the door quickly shut it behind him. There was no one in the place. It was popular with students, no so much with the Sunday dinner crowd; they were most likely all at Furr's Cafeteria. The short woman behind the counter appeared to be in her sixties, with orange hair in a beauty parlor swirl atop her head, beneath a colorful Taco Bueno cap. Her name tag read: RUBY, MANAGER.

"Howdy," she said with a plastic smile, in the high, squeaky drawl of a West Texas woman. "How you doin' today, sir?"

"Fine," Parker replied. "How 'bout yourself?"

"Just peachy. What'll it be?"

"Oh, let's see. I'll take two softshell tacos and a Cherry Coke, to go."

She told him the total, took his money, and said, "Be right up." Then she turned to go back to the food prep area and sneezed, loudly, stopping in her tracks and doubling over. "Didn't make it," she mumbled, probably to herself. She took two more steps and sneezed again, just as violently as before, and disappeared around the corner.

"Wash your hands," said a voice, almost a whisper.

"Huh?" Parker looked down at the other end of the counter and saw a girla pproaching, still buttoning up the shirt of her Taco Bueno uniform. Her long, sandy blond hair was fixed in a ponytail, her bangs hanging down to her eyebrows, just above the patch of freckles splattered across her nose. She looked about Parker's age, and she wore no make-up, which helped her look all the more beautiful.

"Oh, I was just talking to my boss," she said. "Sorta." According to the tag on her chest, her name was Kim. She smiled at Parker, then looked past him, out the windows. "Is it nice out there?"

Parker glanced outside, at the blowing dust. "Oh, not really. Not yet, at least. It's still pretty windy. I've got this warm jacket on, but it still seemed a little chilly to me."

She frowned. "I wish it would warm up. I've been so cold."

"Yeah, me too."

Suddenly her face brightened up. "Do you think it'll be nice by four?"

"I don't know," said Park, thinking *what does she think I am, a meteorologist?* He noticed the way she was looking at him, with a twinkle in her gray eyes, and dimples bracketing her smile. "Is that when you get off? Four?" he asked.

"Yeah. I hope it's nice. I want to go to the park."

With me? Parker wondered. He could never pick up vibes from girls, could never tell when they were just hinting at something, or when they were just being friendly. "Well, the sun is out, and it's usually best around three these days. I bet it'll be nice at four, if the wind's not still blowing."

The girl handed him his bag of food and the drink. "Here y'are. Thanks for the weather tip." She hesitated before letting go of the order, as if she were waiting for something.

Now was his chance. "Hey, when you get off you wouldn't like some company, would you? For going to the park?"

Her eyes lit up. "Sure, that'd be great, uh—"

"Parker," he mumbled.

"Kim." Awkwardly, she gestured at her name tag. "I'll meet you there, about four-fifteen, by the fountain, okay?" She looked over her shoulder nervously.

"Terrific, see you then." He waved as he turned to go.

"I'll be looking forward to it."

When he left Taco Bueno, the wind and dust stung his face, but he didn't care; he had a date. He looked back inside, but now the old lady had returned to the counter, and Kim was gone.

PARKER WAS HALFWAY THROUGH his first taco when he noticed the gritty, abrasive taste. He took the taco away from his mouth and looked at it. Bile rose in his throat. The tortilla was entirely covered with greenish-blue mold and a fuzzy white growth. He dropped the taco, letting it fall onto the table. He spat the half-chewed wad of food onto the paper wrapper in front of him, and continued spitting, trying to get the last of it out of his mouth. In the tiny pile of food he had nearly swallowed, something was squirming. It looked like a worm. Disgusted, he opened up the taco to see what was inside. Withered, black lettuce was piled upon cheese that was green and slimy, and what was supposed to have been ground beef looked instead like gray, radiated flesh, crawling with beetles, worms, and wiggling white maggots.

"Jesus Christ!" he yelled.

It must have been that senile old woman. She probably hadn't washed her hands after she'd sneezed, either.

He ran to the bathroom, knowing he would vomit any second. Glancing in the mirror, he saw his lips were blue from the moldy tortilla. He opened his mouth; his tongue was the same color. He started to gag. Then he was on his knees before the toilet, the ghastly taco coming out of his throat in a long, brown, putrid stream.

HE RETURNED TO TACO BUENO a little after one o'clock, having gargled half a bottle of minty mouthwash. There were several people in the place now: a rancher in a Stetson with his wife and kids, and a gaggle of teenage girls. They were sitting in booths eating burritos, enchiladas, and tacos that looked quite delicious. Parker had brought his bag along with him, with the one-and-a-half rotten tacos inside.

"Howdy!" said the old woman, beaming.

"Howdy, yourself," said Parker bitterly. He felt like calling her all sorts of filthy names, but his better judgment stopped him.

"I thought that was awful funny, you payin' your money and then walkin' out like that, just when I'd got your food ready."

"But that girl gave me my food. It was shit."

The manager stiffened. "What girl?"

"Kim." Parker narrowed his eyes to slits and gave the woman a hard glare. "Sandy hair, gray eyes, freckles, you know."

"I'm sorry, sir." Her face went ashen. "I'm the only one workin' this afternoon."

"Oh yeah?" Parker couldn't believe this bullshit.

"Besides . . . Kim hasn't worked here for two months or more. If this is some kind of joke, I sure don't think it's very funny."

"You're not going to weasel out of it like this, lady. What kind of taco do you think you're making here?"

"Why, I don't know what you mean."

Parker handed her the bag. "Take a look in there," he said raising his voice. "It's disgusting. These tacos made me sick. The cheese was rotten, the meat was—hell, I don't even know if it was beef—the most rancid thing I've ever eaten, crawling with worms, maggots, and God knows what else—"

The rancher and his family raised their heads to see what was going on.

The manager turned the bag upside down and dumped out the contents. All that came out was a huge pile of paper napkins.

"I don't get it," said Parker. "It was—they were—"

The rancher chuckled and went back to eating his taco.

The old woman scowled, and a lock of her curled, orange hair fell out of place across her wrinkled forehead. "I don't get it, either," she said. "Get out of my place. You damned kids and your pranks. Y'all are sick!"

BY THE TIME HE GOT BACK to his apartment, he felt queasy again. He pulled down the shades, turned off the light, and collapsed on the bed. He wondered what had happened to the tacos. They had been right there in the bag, he was sure of it. He had no idea where all those napkins had come from. Maybe the old bitty had switched bags on him while he wasn't looking—a little sleight of hand so she wouldn't get shut down by the Department of Health.

Or maybe the tacos had never really been there to begin with. Maybe he was nuts, or sick like the woman had said.

His stomach churned, and he felt miserably weak. Those tacos had done something to him, he was certain of that. He unfastened his belt buckle and unbuttoned his jeans; there was painful gas in his abdomen, and he was beginning to feel bloated. He couldn't get that awful taste out of his mouth, despoite all the mouthwash he'd used. He kept burping, and the taste kept coming back.

Parker knew he was about to drift off to sleep, so he grabbed his alarm clock and set it to 4:00 P.M. He wasn't about to miss this meeting with Kim. She would have all the answers.

WHEN HE WOKE UP and shut off the beeping alarm, he felt much better, although his joints were stiff. He crawled out of bed and grabbed a clean shirt from the closet, then tucked it in and buttoned up his jeans. He gargled with mouthwash and brushed his teeth until all he could taste was mint, grabbed his jacket, and left.

The wind had died, and the street was calm. A few cars rushed past on the boulevard, but it was nothing compared to the usual traffic when the rest of the students were in town. Parker walked down the street, heading for the park, which was another three blocks, in the opposite direction from Taco Bueno.

There was hardly anyone at the park, either. He saw a few solitary figures walking or sitting or jogging, but not the usual crowds. The vast expanse of grass was yellowish brown in color, criss-crossed by arcing cement walkways, with a fountain at the center. At least the fountain had been turned on, Parker thought.

But Kim wasn't there.

Parker looked at his watch, but it had stopped. Oh well, he figured, it was somehwere around four-fifteen. He decided to go to the fountain and wait for Kim there. He looked up at the tall cottonwoods as he walked by. They had yet to bud, their bare limbs reaching toward the sky, grasping, for something. The shadow of one fell across the fountain in the glaring sunlight of late afternoon. The fountain had a circular base, and two platforms in the center down which the bubbling water cascaded; it was traditional, nothing special at all. People threw pennies in it, and in the summer young children went wading.

He touched the water. It was cool, but he thought it should have felt *cold*.

"Wash your hands." Kim's voice came from behind him.

He turned around with a start. "Oh, Kim!" He grinned, embarrassed. "I didn't see you coming."

"Hi, Parker."

She was captivating in the warm glow of the sun. The light glinted off her fine hair, which now hung loose over her shoulders, to her breasts. She wore well-fitting jeans and a yellow button-up blouse. Her smile showed she was now the embarrassed one, under the scrutiny of Parker's long, silent gaze. The light breeze blew some of her hair in her face, which she tossed back with a jerk of her head. Something about her made Parker feel good, deep down.

"No, wait, don't move. Just stand right like that for a minute."

She laughed. "What for?"

"I like how you look in the sunlight."

"Really? Then why don't you come stand here with me, in the light? Let's see how you look."

Parker walked over, and stood in front of her. "There."

"Oh, nice." She put her hand up to her chin and regarded him, first the left side, then the right. "Very nice. Yeah, you're cute."

Parker wanted to say, "You're beautiful," but somehow the words didn't come out. Things had never moved this fast with a girl before. He wanted to kiss her, but knew she probably wouldn't let him. Then the taco sprang back into his mind.

"Why the frown?" Kim asked, sounding disappointed.

"Kim, how well do you know the lady you work for?"

"Ruby, you mean? At Taco Bueno? Oh, I don't work there anymore."

"That's what she told me, that you hadn't worked there for two months. So what were you doing there today?"

Kim put her arms around Parker's back and squeezed his obliques. "Maybe I wanted to meet you."

"I don't understand." He put his arms around her, and held her close against him while looking down into her gray eyes. "You're cold."

"So are you."

"Do you know what was in those tacos you handed me?"

"Yes," she said with a smirk. "I made them."

With that, she kissed Parker full on the lips. Feeling dizzy, he closed his eyes, and his mouth parted to receive her tongue. Her kiss was powerful, and he could feel it somehow changing them both. Then he tasted the moldy grit, the foul meat, the rotten decay of the taco. Maggots squirmed into his mouth. He broke the kiss gasping for air, and spat the horrible things from his mouth, but he coulnd't get rid of the *taste*.

He opened his eyes and looked at Kim's face. What was left of her skin was gray and flaky, but mostly she was a putrefied mass of blackened jelly clinging to a skull, with ratty, knotted hair streaming down from the scalp, framing her wide, cadaverous grin.

Parker backed away. "Y-you're dead!" he shouted.

The corpse laughed, and said, "Look who's talking."

Frantic, Parker whirled around and looked once, briefly, at his reflection in the water of the fountain, and saw his worm-eaten face. Then he knew.

Kim leaned over him. "I'm so glad I found you."

Telling Tales

———

"ARE YOU NERVOUS?" the prosecutor asked me, flipping a lock of hair out of her eyes. Yesterday's papers had criticized her hairdo, and since then she'd somehow found time to get a new one. It didn't seem to me much of an improvement. Now she was staring right at me, and I had to buck myself up by remembering what my attorney told me: *The old man is gone, OK? She's your enemy now. She's the one with the evil eye. You got it, kid?*

"Yes," I said, leaning into the mike, my hands coiling and uncoiling the supple rubber cord. I had reason to be nervous. I was on trial for murder in the first degree, live and uncensored in front of the whole world on Court TV, and it was my first time on television.

"That's all right," she said soothingly. "It's all right."

"But I'm not mad," I added. I glanced over at my attorney to see if I was doing OK. He was wincing like he had heartburn.

"May I remind the court," said the prosecutor, sighing for effect—*oh, she's good, she's very clever—this case is going to make her a star*—"that the defendant has already been found competent to stand trial and that no one here is questioning either his sanity or his ability to testify on his own behalf."

"Noted," said the judge—*smarmy bastard, I'd like to stand up and slap that smirk off his face.* "Proceed."

"You've already admitted to killing the old man."

"Yes, ma'am, that's correct." I swallowed hard.

"Yet you've also stated that you loved him."

"Yes, ma'am."

"Why?"

"Excuse me?"

"Why did you love him?"

"He took me off the streets. I'd been living at the Port Authority bus terminal with a bunch of other kids, but we hardly had anything to eat. Then one day this old man comes up and asks me if I want a job taking care of him, and I says, 'Sure.' Of course I loved him. He saved my life, maybe."

"And how did you pay him back?"

"Excuse me?"

"With a knife in the back, isn't that right? Isn't that how you paid him back for all the things he did for you?"

"Objection!" my attorney shouted, standing up, just like on *Perry Mason*.

"Overruled," said the judge.

"That's not true," I said. "It wasn't a knife. It was a bed."

"Of course it was," the prosecutor said. "That was just a figure of speech. The record already shows that you admit to killing the old man. It's also true that the old man was not stabbed with a knife but crushed beneath an overturned bed."

"Proceed with the questioning," the judge directed. *Yes, exactly, let's stick to the point, Ms. Prosecutor.*

"Is this how people who love one another treat each other?" she asked. This question sounded like a trick.

"Um," I said, biting my bottom lip, looking at my lap, screwing up my eyes. My hand tightened on the microphone cord. *When in doubt,* my attorney had told me, *just cry.* I was trying now, but no tears came. I stared back up at the prosecutor, right into her eyes. "I never wanted to. He made me do it."

"How did he make you do it?"

"With . . . with—" I bit my lip again and strained to cry.

The sweater my attorney had made me wear was itching and scratching at me, and it was hot in the courtroom. My vision fogged up, and when I blinked, a couple of tears eked out.

"With what?" she prompted.

"With his evil eye."

"Let me make sure I understand you correctly. You say that it was his evil eye that made you kill him?"

I paused a long time, allowing my lip to tremble, the tears to flow a little more. "Y-yes," I said quietly.

"Please speak into the microphone," the judge said.

I leaned forward and bawled out, "Yes!" looking up at the room. Then I sat back against the chair, heaving with sobs— or trying to, anyway. My attorney was going to be proud of me.

"Can you tell us what you mean by his 'evil eye'?"

"It was just the way he looked at me, most of the time."

"How did he look at you?"

"Like he wanted to rape me."

"Isn't it true that you were his lover?"

"Houseboy," I said. "He hired me to clean his house, cook his meals, and take care of him. He didn't hire me to have sex with him. At least, that's what I thought."

"But you and he did have sex on a number of occasions, didn't you?"

"Well, yes," I said. "But he made me."

"How did he make you?"

"With his evil eye," I said.

The prosecutor sighed in exasperation. She hated those two words, I could tell. "Did he ever threaten you?"

"Not at first," I said. "Not directly."

"You stated on the record that every time you and the old man had sex, it was rape, that you told him you didn't want to do it. Perhaps you'd care to share with the court just how this so-called evil eye could force you to have nonconsensual sex with him?"

"Well, he would just look at you, and you'd have no choice but to do what he wanted," I said.

"Do you expect us to believe this was some kind of hypnosis?"

"No," I said, laughing a little. My hand let go of the microphone cord. "But I knew that if I didn't do what he wanted, he would throw me back out on the street and I'd probably starve to death or something. So when he looked at me like that, I'd tell him I didn't want to—"

"How did you tell him?"

"I'd say, 'No, please don't. I don't want to have sex with you. Please don't hurt me.' Stuff like that."

"And what would he do?"

"Oh, he'd just stare at me with that evil eye, and then he'd start touching me, and I'd say, 'No, please don't touch me, I don't want you to touch me like that, please stop,' but he'd just keep on staring at me, and I knew I was going to lose my job if I didn't do whatever he wanted."

"How often did this happen?"

"Every day," I said. "Sometimes twice a day."

"And you claim that every time you and the old man had sex, it was rape, and that you never gave your consent?"

I smiled. She was getting it right. I leaned forward and spoke very clearly and distinctly into the microphone: "Yes, ma'am, that's absolutely the truth."

"And how long were you employed by the old man?"

"Two years, ma'am."

"So, then, it is your testimony that the old man raped you at least once a day for two years?"

"Yes."

"That would be at least seven hundred times."

"If you say so." I shrugged.

"And you expect us to believe that?"

"Objection!" shouted my attorney.

"Sustained," droned the judge.

"And yet you never once went to the police or told anyone about this, this constant rape situation?" the prosecutor asked.

"The cops wouldn't have believed me, and I don't have any friends or family, really. Besides, I would have lost my job, and it was a pretty good gig."

"The old man had money, did he?"

"Yes, ma'am."

"But you've stated on the record that you didn't kill him for the money, is that correct?"

"Oh, yes."

"Yet the old man had named you as sole beneficiary in his will, which meant you stood to inherit over eight hundred thousand dollars as well as the brownstone on West 79th Street here in Manhattan, just off the park—the place the two of you shared. Is that correct?"

"I didn't know nothing about that."

"You have also stated that it was not a, shall we say, crime of passion, but that you killed him only because of this so-called evil eye. Is that correct?"

"Yes." I swallowed hard and tried to express concern in my face by squeezing my eyebrows together and raising them up. I clamped my lips together and nodded my head up and down.

"Would you care to explain to us how the old man's 'evil eye' could have caused you to kill him?"

"Sure," I said. *Now we're getting to the nitty-gritty.* My attorney sat up suddenly in his seat as if he'd just woken up from a nice nap. He clasped his fingers together on the desk and gave me the signal by scratching a supposed itch on the back of his hand.

I glanced over at the Court TV camera and noted that the red light was still on. Everyone was sitting at home all tensed up, waiting to hear the real story, waiting for the good part— the violence, the blood, the kill, the enchilada.

"He'd had enough of me," I explained, breaking into a sob. "He didn't want me anymore. He had this rigid standard of what he liked in a boy. He'd hired me when I was eighteen, and I'd just turned twenty. I was too old for him. He'd used me up and was ready to throw me away. He'd already started going back out—when he felt up to it—and roaming around the Port Authority, looking for new blood. I know. I followed him."

"And how did this make you feel?"

"Mad," I said, then hurried to correct myself. "Not *crazy* mad or nothing, because I'm *not mad*, you know, just *angry* mad."

"I understand," she said in that soothing voice again. She reminded me now of the court shrink who'd talked to me on other occasions. Her eyes kept drilling into me, like vulture's eyes, like the old man's eye. "Go on, I didn't mean to interrupt."

"Thank you." I wiped the sweat from my brow and took a sip of water from the tiny glass before me, careful not to spill it on the microphone. Wouldn't want it to short out right in the middle of my big moment on nationwide TV.

"If you'd like to take a break—"

"No, ma'am," I said, "I'd really like to finish."

"Go ahead."

"Where was I?" She had interrupted my train of thought, and I'd forgotten where I was in my tale.

"You kept following the old man to the bus terminal."

"Yes, thank you. Anyway, now whenever he looked at me, I knew what he was thinking. He wanted to kill me."

"How did you know the old man wanted to kill you?"

"He said so."

"What were his exact words, do you remember?"

"Well, you see, he knew that what he done to me was wrong . . . molesting me like that every day, making me do whatever he wanted, humiliating me like that . . . but he was what they call 'in the closet,' and he didn't want anyone to know what he done to me. So sometimes he would just give me the evil eye and say something like, 'If you ever tell anybody about this, so help me I'll kill you.'"

"Did you take these supposed threats seriously?"

"Of course," I said. "I was frightened for my safety."

"So on the night in question, it has been your testimony that you thought the old man was about to kill you, correct?"

"Yes, that's right."

"What made you think that?"

"He'd told me I was fired and I should pack up my bags and leave the next morning. He was hiring someone new, someone younger, smoother. He said he was tired of me."

"And you interpreted that to mean that he wanted to kill you?"

"Objection, your honor!" said my attorney. "Prosecution is leading the witness."

"Sustained," the judge said. "Prosecutor, please rephrase your question."

"What specifically did he say to you that made you think he wanted to kill you?"

I leaned into the microphone, and my fingers began stroking the black insulation. "He told me I was being let go and if I ever told anyone about him, he was going to kill me."

"Was there any witness to this statement?"

"No."

"So you had been fired. Did this make you upset?"

"Not really. But I was upset that he wanted to kill me."

"You've testified already that you and the old man went to bed that night at around the same time. But you couldn't sleep. Would you please tell the court what happened after that?"

"He came into my room."

"Who came into your room?"

"The old man came into my room, and I woke up, but I still pretended to be asleep. I made it look like my eyes were still closed, but I could see him standing there in the moonlight, staring at me with his evil eye. And I got scared."

"Was he threatening you?"

"Yes, with his eye."

"Was he holding anything in his hands?"

"No. Then he left, but I knew he would be back."

"Why did you think that?"

"He was just looking in to make sure I was asleep. Then he was going to come back and kill me."

"Go on. Guide us through. Tell us what happened."

"I was a wreck. I thought, *I've got to do something, or I'm going to die!* And I knew that I'd better act fast, or he'd be back with an ax or something. So I got up and walked very carefully to his bedroom. Oh, you should have seen how cautious I was! I opened his door carefully—inch by inch—and stepped lightly so I wouldn't wake him up."

"I thought you said he had just visited your room and was just about to kill you," said the prosecutor.

"Let me finish!" I snapped. This would be good, I thought, and would show how much strain I was under, would make the members of the jury all the more sympathetic. *If you win their hearts,* my attorney had said, *we can get this thing knocked down to second-degree—hell, kid, maybe even manslaughter.*

"Go on," said the prosecutor, resigned. Her eyes dimmed

a little.

I was in control now, before all the world. "The old man always kept his room very dark, so I'd brought a flashlight. I needed to make sure he was really there in bed, you see, and not hiding behind the door. So I flicked it on, but the switch made a loud *click!* and he sprang awake, saying, 'Who's there?' I shut it off and left him staring around the darkness. I stood still, not making a peep. I stood like that for an hour, and the old man stayed sitting up in bed, listening, and wouldn't go back to sleep. It was so quiet, I could hear his heart beating, like a watch ticking. Finally, I decided I'd better get it over with before he killed me, so I switched the flashlight back on, and the light landed right on his evil eye!"

I paused, waiting for her to ask another question, but she just stood there staring at me. I assumed that she wanted me to continue. My attorney had told me not to talk so much and not to talk unless asked a question, but I couldn't stop myself now.

"It was him or me," I said, "so I came at him, dragged him out of bed, and pulled the bed over on top of him. His heart kept beating for a while. I could hear it, but it was muffled by the bed. Then it stopped. He was dead, and so was his eye."

"And you are claiming that it was self-defense, correct?"

"Yes, ma'am."

"You state that the old man was about to kill you, and that you had no other choice, is that your testimony?"

"Yes, that's it." I smiled eagerly at her. She was getting it right, finally. But suddenly she came forward, placing either hand on the witness stand, and stared down at me with those eyes of hers. She was blocking the TV cameras. Her eyes were intimidating, and instinctively I shrunk down in my seat, remembering how the old man had used his eyes to make me do his bidding.

The old man is gone, OK? She's your enemy now. She's the one with the evil eye. You got it, kid?

"Yes," I mumbled. I peered over the prosecutor's shoulder to get a glimpse of my attorney. He gave me an encouraging nod that said to me, *don't give up now, give her all you've got.*

"Then tell me *why,*" the prosecutor screamed at me, "why, if this was an act of self-defense, you would go to the trouble of *dismembering* the corpse, *cutting off the head and limbs,* tearing up the flooring, and *hiding* the bloody body parts under the *planks?* I'd like to hear you try to explain that!"

"There was no blood on the body," I corrected her. "The tub caught it all."

"I thought you said the *evil eye* was *dead.* It couldn't have told you to cut him up, could it? It couldn't have told you to hide the body, could it? Because it was dead! The old man was dead! You *murdered* him in *cold blood* and then tried to cover it up. And you almost got away with it, didn't you? Except that you *admitted* it to the police! You tore up the floor yourself and told them the *whole thing!*"

"Objection, your honor," said the attorney. "I would remind the court that the defendant recanted his confession, which was made under duress and is not part of the evidence in this trial."

"Sustained," said the judge. "Strike the prosecutor's comments from the record. And I would warn you against making further references to matters this court has deemed irrelevant."

Oh, this made her mad! She was standing there over me

like some bird of prey eyeing her kill. She wanted to get me. She was my enemy, all right. My attorney knew all along.

"The fact is," said the prosecutor, breathing heavily now and staring right into my eyes. She was so close, I could hear her little bird heart beating. "The fact of the matter is, the old man was perfectly harmless. Our medical experts have testified that there is no evidence you were ever forced to have sex, and the court psychiatrist has testified that you do not fit the psychological profile of someone who has been raped even once, let alone seven hundred times. The fact of the matter is, you stood to inherit nearly a million dollars in cold, hard cash, plus a choice piece of Manhattan real estate — you, who until you met the old man had been sleeping in the dingy corridors of a rat-infested bus terminal! The fact of the matter is, you murdered the old man in a horrible, violent act that was cold and premeditated. The fact of the matter is, you acted to hide all evidence that any murder had even taken place. *And you came this close to getting away with it. Isn't that right?*"

This last bit she whispered at me, but I'm sure it was picked up on the microphone and carried over the cable lines to the living rooms of millions of housewives and unemployed people. She was holding her fingers together, demonstrating that I had come within a hair's breadth of success. And she was right.

If I didn't act fast, I was going to let my attorney down, and I couldn't do that — not after everything he'd done for me.

Before the prosecutor knew what was happening, I was yanking the mike out of its holder, looping the cord around her neck, and pulling her head down into the witness box. I tightened the cord with a quick yank. Her new hairdo fell in her face. The judge was pounding his gavel and calling for the deputies. The prosecutor looked up at me, and her evil eyes bulged out of her sockets. Her heart beat faster and faster and then, suddenly, stopped.

As the deputies dragged me from the stand, I glanced over at my attorney. The camera and all eyes in the courtroom were trained on me, so he was in no danger of being seen.

His eyes had gone misty, and his smile had gone greedy, and he very discreetly gave me a big fat thumbs-up.

THE STRAWBERRY MAN

———

TENNY AND ANDRÉ WERE CRUISING along the sidewalk on their skateboards when they caught sight of the old man. Tenny had been staring so intently at André's ass twisting and turning ahead of him that he might never have noticed the man, if it hadn't been for the shiny aluminum hardhat he was wearing. The old man was dressed in work clothes selling strawberries, the sun's bright reflection beaming from his silvery hat, right into Tenny's eyes.

"Hey, André!" Tenny shouted, bringing himself to a halt near the entrance of a gravel road. "Hold up." Tenny flipped his skateboard up under his arm; it was carved all over with the names of his favorite bands.

André stopped and asked, "What for, man?" He bent over to pick up the skateboard, his cut-off sweatpants riding up the cleft of his ass cheeks.

The sun shone brilliantly through an open patch of blue, but was about to be enveloped by the low-hanging, dark storm clouds that covered most of the sky. Tenny and André both dripped with sweat, their shorts and t-shirts clinging to their skin from the oppressive mugginess of the afternoon. They were out of breath, and thirsty.

The gravel road stretched into the woods and over the hill, to the strawberry fields, where anyone could go pick their own fresh for a small fee.

"Look," said Tenny, pointing at the man.

Two ancient oak trees were stationed on either side of the gravel road, providing ample shade. Yet the man had parked his pickup truck out away from the trees, closer to the sidewalk, and was sitting on the open tailgate in the direct sunlight, where he sorted out piles of freshly picked strawberries and put them in green, quart-sized containers. His plump figure entirely filled the large pair of overalls that he wore over a white short-sleeved t-shirt. The dark sunglasses sitting on his pudgy, sunburnt face hid his eyes completely from view. The hardhat he wore on his head looked incredibly uncomfortable in the damp heat. As he worked, he ate his own strawberries noisily, his fat double chin bobbing up and down as he chewed.

"Howdy, boys," said the man with a grin. His aging teeth displayed a pinkish tint.

Now he was twenty-one, Tenny no longer appreciated being called a boy6, but he supposed his spiked hair and ragged t-shirt, André's mohawk and multiple earrings, as well as their skateboards, made them both seem immature to this old guy.

"Here, boys, free samples," said the man, and handed them two apiece. "Freshest strawbrerries you'll ever eat."

Tenny looked up at the strawberries piled up in the bed of

the pickup, and examined the two in his hand more closely. They were perfect in every respect, a bright glossy red, over two inches long, their round tapered shape as balanced as a top, and capped with a small leafy crown and a slightly curved stem. They were prime examples of strawberries, good enough for an advertisement, and certainly good enough to eat.

Tenny held his strawberries up to André's face. "Just look at them. They're beautiful!"

Tenny bit into one. The sweet, tangy flavor flooded his taste buds with delight. André sat nibbling his.

"Looks like rain, I'd say," said the old man.

"Mmm. Delicious," said Tenny. He bought a whole quart, promising André he would share them with him.

The sun disappeared behind a cloud, and a low rumbling could be heard in the distance. The air smelled like rain. It could start to pour any minute, Tenny figured.

"Thanks, guy," said Tenny to the old man.

The man's cheery red face smiled back at them. "No, thank you. Bye now, fellas. Come on back."

"Sure," said André. Then to Tenny: "Give me a few of those."

"Come on, let's get back to the apartment. It's going to soak us in a few seconds." They hopped on their skateboards and started off. Tenny carried the quart of strawberries with his left hand, tucking it under his arm.

A flash of lightning lit up the gray sky, followed soon after by an earth-shattering crack of thunder.

Tenny glanced back over his shoulder, and saw the man was gone. He did a double take. The man must have wanted to beat the rain, but he couldn't possibly have gotten away so quickly.

"Hey, watch it!"

Tenny looked ahed just in time to find himself running smack into André. They fell off their boards and landed together on the grass in a heap. Tenny's face ended up in André's armpit, where he got a good whiff of his musk, while his thigh landed in André's crotch, nearly racking him. The strawberries went flying, most of them landing in the gutter or the street.

"Get off of me, you slut," said André.

Tenny got up and grabbed his skateboard from nearby, where it had struck a chain-link fence. A car zoomed by, squishing several strawberries beneath its tires.

It started to rain.

"Fucking hell," said Tenny.

IT WAS RAINING AGAIN the next day by the time Tenny woke up. He put a Revolting Cocks disc in the CD player, opened up a can of Meister Brau for himself, and sat down with the Chicago Sun-Times. André came out from the bedroom naked, scratching the stubbly scalp beneath his mohawk and yawning. "Morning," he stated.

"Afternoon," said Tenny, grinning at André slyly.

"Shit."

"Stud."

"Slut." André's eyes were bleary, but he looked good. His upper body was solidly built, and he had taut, well-muscled drummer's arms. He was part of a band called Mach Twang that played industrial dance music verging on speedmetal, and he channeled all of his energy into his drumming. There wasn't an ounce of fat on his body, since it was all sweated off in their rehearsals and occasional gigs. Whatever energy he had left over Tenny received in the form of a hard cock up his butt.

"Let's see if that strawberry guys is out again today," said André, opening his beer.

"You read my mind," said Tenny. André often did, they had known each other so long. "Oh, you got some mail. Your student loan went through." Tenny handed him the letter from the bank.

"Cooler than shit! Not a word to my folks."

"Nada." Tenny couldn't tell André's parents because André wasn't going to return to school come September. Instead, he was going to put most of the money in the band fund. Any money Mach Twang was making now was negligible; on some gigs they made money, on some they lost, and it turned out even. Yet they had expenses to cover—renting the PA, paying the sound company, not to mention transportation. They needed money, and all the band members were pitching in. André was going to contribute his student loan. He only hoped the band could land a contract with Wax Trax or some other independent label before his parents found out he had dropped out of school. Luckily, the lived a thousand miles away and wouldn't know any better.

"We'll just have to celebrate," said André. "Let's go get some strawberries."

They went on their skateboards, through the pelting rain, to the entrance of the gravel road where the old man had been the day before. But there was nothing there except the two old oak trees, their leave sfluttering in the wind and rain. It rained all day long, and the man selling strawberries was nowhere to be found.

* * *

THE RAIN CLEARED UP the following morning, and by noon with the sun out the temperature had reached ninety-one degrees, with 74-percent humidity, according to the clerk at the 7-Eleven, where Tenny had gone to buy beer.

They found the man where he had been before, sitting on the tailgate of his pickup truck in the bright sun. His red face greeted them with a smile, his hardhat and sunglasses reflecting the sun into their eyes.

"How did you like 'em, boys?" asked the man.

Tenny laughed, embarrassed. "We didn't get to eat any. I accidentally tossed them in the street. That's why we're back."

"Well, I daresay I got myself a better batch today, anyhow. They've been sitting here just waiting for some good folk like yourselves to come along and — "

"I'm Tenny, and this is André," he said, offering his hand. The old man shook hands with him, leaving Tenny's pink and sticky and smelling of strawberries.

André shook hands with him, too, but seemed impatient. "We'll take two quarts this time. We only want your best."

"Got 'em right here." The man showed them two quarts of freshly picked strawberries like none they had ever seen. Each strawberry was perfect in shape, color, texture, smell, as if hand-crafted by gods. Tenny and André each grabbed a quart for themselves. André handed the man some bills, and the man gave him his change.

"You out here every day?" asked André, setting down his skateboard and placing one foot upon it.

"Whenever the sun shines and the sky is blue, yessir. For one more week, then I move on."

Tenny hopped on his skateboard and asked, "You got a name, guy?"

The man popped a strawberry in his mouth and began to chew. "Oh, I'm just the Strawberry Man," he said. "It was nice making your acquaintance."

Tenny and André looked at each other puzzledly, and Tenny shrugged and said, "Okay."

"C'mon, slut, let's blow."

They blew.

THEY DUMPED THE STRAWBERRIES together in a large bowl, and set them on the kitchen table.

"Wow!" said André. "Look at them."

"Incredible," muttered Tenny, mostly to himself. "Go ahead."

André hesitated, then reached for the topmost strawberry and quickly devoured it. "Your turn."

Tenny took one and stared at it for a moment, looking for a flaw—a bruise, a nick, a discoloration, anything. But there was none. He couldn't resist any longer, and promptly ate it. It was the most divine taste he had ever encountered.

From that point on, it was almost a race. Tenny and André sat down and munched strawberries one after the other like two chain smokers getting their nicotine fix. They made grunts and groans of pleasure, licked their fingers like little boys, and barely allowed any time to savor the flavor of one strawberry before putting the next in their mouths. Tenny's heart beat faster with excitement as the bowl became further depleted. His taste buds were so satisfied, he was getting an erection. Tenny wondered if perhaps he had found a legitimate aphrodisiac, but quickly realized that idea was mistaken; he felt like making love, yes, but not to André—to a *strawberry*.

Suddenly, a car horn blared loudly outside.

"Oh, shit!" said André, looking at his watch. "It's three o'clock. I'm supposed to take some ad copy down to the newspaper for our gig tomorrow night, and do some postering. Rick's going to take me into the city. I've got to go."

"You'll be a few hours or so?"

"Yeah," said André, grabbing a manila folder from beside the phone. He took a handful of strawberries, looked suspiciously at Tenny, gave him a kiss, and added, "Save half of those for me or you die."

After first putting on a Ministry CD and cranking the sound, Tenny moved the bowl of strawberries to the coffee table in the living room and shoved the alternative music magazines and assorted independent rags to the floor. Then he sorted the berries into two piles, separate but equal.

He decided he would only eat from his own pile, and leave the others for André, his fair share after all. He chewed sweet, juicy chunks of strawberry flesh, and his senses tingled. With his eyes closed, he couldn't help but sit there grinning stupidly while the juicy nectar slid down his throat. He was in heaven.

Before long, he was down to his last strawberry. He held it in between thumb and forefinger and considered it, rolling it back and forth. He bit the tip off it, and glanced nervously at the coffee table. André's considerable pile of strawberries sat there, tempting him.

But he was determined not to eat André's strawberries. He would have to make the most of what he had.

Where he had already taken a bite, Tenny smeared the strawberry across his lips, an electric sensation along the sensitive, chapped skin. Tenny hopped to his feet, went into the bathroom, and stood before the mirror. A glossy pinkish stain coated his mouth. He took the strawberry and rubbed it on the skin beneath his cheekbones, and turned his head so he could see a three-quarter view of himself. *Damn, he looked good!* He rubbed the strawberry across his eyelids. *Perfect.* He put a pink streak in his blond, spiked hair. *Too fucking cool.* He threw off his t-shirt and pressed the strawberry against one nipple, then the ohter. This was too much; he was getting an erection again. He squeezed the strawberry and let a pink trickle of juice flow down his chest. Then, finally, he couldn't resist any longer, and ate it.

André's return was still an hour or two away.

Tenny went back to the living room. There was no way he could hold out until André got back. The pile sat waiting in the bowl, a brilliant red treasure upon the dull, dusty coffee table.

"Methinks thou dost mock me," said Tenny aloud, irreverently, before sitting down and eating them.

TENNY WAS DRUNK when André entered the apartment. Crushed cans of Meister Brau were strewn about, and the old, scratched Killing Joke CD he had just put on was skipping, arbitrarily spitting out snatches of primal drum beats at random to Tenny's pleasure and amusement. From his seat on the couch, Tenny smiled at André and offered him the last of his beer, clutched shakily in his hand.

André looked at the empty bowl on the coffee table and frantically glanced in the kitchen. Tenny half expected to see steam purging from his ears, then laughed uncontrollably at the thought.

"Where are my strawberries?" demanded André.

Tenny pointed to his own mouth. "Sorry, stud, I couldn't help it. They were too good."

André's face was rigid. He rushed over to the couch and looked intently at Tenny's face. Then, suddenly André kissed him firmly on the lips, poking his tongue into Tenny's mouth and swirling it around, exploring every corner. Tenny was too stunned, as well as too drunk, to think. André had looked more like he was about to hit him than kiss him. But at last, André broke the kiss, scowling.

"Damn," he said. "All I can taste is beer."

"So what?"

"I don't give a shit about turning you on. I'm just looking for some strawberry."

ABOVE THE ENTRANCE to the ancient, soot-blackened brick warehouse, the sign read:

THE OVENS
entre at yr owne ryske

in blue and pink neon. Green photocopied posters advertising tonight's show, with ("Chicago's own") Baby Spiders opening up for ("suburban snots") Mach Twang, were plastered outside the entrance beneath two bright, bare light bulbs. Tenny stumbled up the crumbling cement steps to the door, and smirked at the bouncer. He didn't have to tell the guy he was on the guest list for Mach Twang. He was known here, and was never any trouble. Even though he didn't need to have his hand stamped, he asked to have it done anyway, because he liked to have proof that he was a nifty guy.

Tenny had felt moody, depressed, and shaky ever since the previous evening, after he had eaten the last of the strawberries. At least being drunk had helped. But now that he was dry, with a hangover to boot, he felt like shit. Purple, puffy bags hung beneath his eyes, and his muscles were tied up in knots. His mind was all goofy; he couldn't tell if the stamp on his hand was a dragon's head or the letter G.

Baby Spiders were already thrashing away on stage, and a small group of people were slam-dancing all over the floor. Many were wearing severely distressed pairs of jeans, with white t-shirts and leather jackets. The bodies bounced off one another in an ecstatic blur. But there weren't yet enough people out there for it to be any fun.

The smoke-filled interior of the Ovens was done in black and white, with café-style iron tables and chairs circling the floor in two terraced levels surrounding the stage. The gray walls were lit with subdued lights of varied color shooting upwards from the floor. Plastic plants throughout were spray-painted an ashen tone. Poseurs, punks, a few hippies and rastafarians, and other assorted types crowded around the tables everywhere, talking and smoking while they avidly downed their drinks.

Tenny went to the bar and bought a Rolling Rock. He took a large gulp, his hand shaking uncontrollably. He was eager to get drunk, to rid himself of this desperate craving for the old man's strawberries. He hadn't been able to eat all day, because his stomach wouldn't take anything else; the hot dog he had eaten at lunch had immediately come right back out. He could recall how the strawberries had tasted, but this only made it worse, and did nothing to satisfy his desire.

Tenny stepped out in between bands for a breath of fresh air. By this time, The Ovens had filled up and was teeming with warm, sweaty bodies. He sat on the steps smoking a cigarette, and he couldn't believe his eyes when he saw, parked in the shadows on the other side of the street, the pickup truck belonging to the Strawberry Man.

He dashed across the street, absently letting his cigarette fall from his lips. The pickup smelled wonderful, but there were no strawberries in either the bed or the cab; all he could see through the grimy windows were red stains on the white vinyl bench seat. In any case, the truck was locked. Tenny glanced around anxiously, looking up and down the street, but saw no sign of the Strawberry Man.

André must have invited him to the gig.

Taking one last whiff of the strawberry-mobile, Tenny grinned with anticipation and raced back into the club.

Mach Twang's gear was all set up on the stage, so it was clear they were about to go on. Bessie, one of the waitresses, was going about from table to table, setting aluminum pie plates at each one; they were filled with strawberries.

"Courtesy of Mach Twang," the girl intoned at every stop. "Courtesy of Mach Twa—"

Tenny grabbed a handful out of the tin she was holding.

"Go ahead, Tenny," she said. "They're free."

"Fucking incredible," he said, popping two in his mouth. "Where'd you get them?"

"Your friends—" said Bessie, munching on a strawberry. "'Scuse me. Your friends brought them. They're in the dungeon."

Finishing his wad of strawberries, Tenny pushed through

the crowd and opened the door near the stage that led to the basement. He rushed down the steep, rickety stairs, tripping down the last two steps, the result of too many beers.

"Ain't it cool, Tenny? Ain't it?" André leapt from his seat on a box of wine coolers when he saw Tenny. He grabbed several strawberries from a nearby tin and started feeding them to Tenny, shoving them one by one into his mouth. Gene, Travis, and Fred, the rest of Mach Twang, laughed while they stood around eating. Their faces were stark and shadowy in the harsh light of the single hanging bulb.

"Mmmph!" Tenny tried to speak. "Gmmgmmph." He put his hands up and waved frantically to get André to stop stuffing berries down his throat.

"Sorry, Tenny."

Tenny chewed them up and swallowed them in a few big gulps. "Jeez, how'd you get so many?"

"I bought them." André kissed him, both of their lips sticky with strawberry juice, their tongues slippery sweet.

Of course, with his loan André had beaucoup bucks.

"I saw the Strawberry Man's truck —" Tenny looked about the room, which was nothing more than a supply room, small and damp, with stone walls, filled with boxes of booze. At this club, it was the only private place a band could have to themselves before going on stage. Atop the stacks of boxes, everywhere, were more plates of strawberries than Tenny could count. "So where is he?"

André motioned drunkenly at the closed door on the opposite wall. "In there, that little room. He stashed his strawberries there when he came." A sign on the door said: DO NOT DISTURB.

"I didn't see him come in the club," said Tenny.

"Neither did we," said Fred. "He was here when we came down, after Baby Spiders was done."

The door opened a crack, and the Strawberry Man's arm set a new, full pan alongside several others on a case of beer. Then the door slammed shut.

"Guys," said Gene, "we gotta go. C'mon. Travis, got the song list?"

"Mmmph," said Travis.

"Here," said André, handing Tenny his own personal plate of strawberries. "Enjoy. See you after."

Tenny popped a berry into his mouth. After the band had left the dungeon, he thought of opening the door across the room and saying hello to the Strawberry Man, but something held him back. He turned and bounded up the stairs, being careful not to spill his plate.

BY THE TIME MACH TWANG had finished their seventh song, everybody in The Ovens was munching on strawberries. The pie plates were all over, on tables, bannisters, bar stools, and at the edge of the stage; there was plenty. Grinning teeth glistened through the dim light. Self-absorbed mods were licking sticky juice off their fingers, while pretty poseurs licked each other's. Even the punks were emerging from the pool of jerking limbs and thrashing mohawks ever so often to grab more handfuls of strawberries, which they put in their jacket pockets and ate while they slammed.

Tenny ate quickly, listening to the deafening roar of distortion. The machine-gun rapid pounding and beating of André's drums penetrated his body as deeply as did André's prick when they were in bed. He wanted desperately to plunge into the crowd and join the slam-dancing. But he couldn't until his plate was finished.

The band was playing one of the first songs they had written, "Mary Mace":

> *My mom was CIA Mary Mace*
> *Never let go of her leatherette briefcase . . .*

Something was wrong.

Tenny looked all around the club, at the hundreds of people eating strawberries. He wondered what the hell was so special about these things, why they were so delicious, and why it was impossible to stop eating them or, after tasting them, to eat anything else. They were not ordinary. Something was definitely wrong.

Fred, the singer and guitarist, announced into the microphone, "We just wrote this: 'Discombobulated.'" The band let loose right away. The beat was fast, furious, ideal for slam-dancing. The guitars cut a jagged rhythm, while Travis's slick synthesizer tracks wailed high above in a frenzied intro. Gene's throbbing bass and André's frenetic drumming meshed together, sounding like an old heavy-duty washing machine in the spin cycle.

> *Nervous, little, agitated*
> *Now you're incarcerated . . .*

Tenny was down to a handful of strawberries. He twisted the pie plate into a ball and threw it at Fred's head: it bounced off Fred's ear and landed on the stage. Tenny held tightly onto the last of his berries and went out onto the dance floor. He pushed his way through the leather, denim, pale skin, haircuts, and sideburns until he was where the action was. Then it was out of control. He was shoving, being pushed and punched, throwing his clenched fists around, banging up against countless bodies . . .

Feeble and frustrated
They want you eradicated . . .

He popped some strawberries into his mouth. Someone slammed up against him, forcing him to bite his tongue. He could taste the blood swirling in his mouth with the strawberry juice. He spat. The watery pink mixture hit the nape of a skinhead's neck, just below his swastika tattoo, and then suddenly three or four bodies thrust into the space between Tenny and the skinhead, before the skinhead disappeared into the crowd, just another pretty face, gone forever. Tenny was being spun around, letting the crowd dictate his movements. He was shoved up against the stage, his ribcage squeezed in by a mass of punks, and then the pressure was gone, and he was flying back into the swirl of arms and poking elbows. He shoved against a couple guys, then slipped on the beer-slick floor, but was quickly helped back up by nine reaching, grabbing arms. The last of his strawberries were scattered on the floor; people were picking them up, some getting their fingers stomped on, but they didn't seem to care. They gobbled them up, smiling . . .

Thanks Pigs Incroporated . . .

"Hey, Goddammit!" Tenny shouted, but of course no one heard him above the music. He caught a glimpse of Bessie's face going past in a blur. "Hey!" he thrust his way through and grabbed her shoulder. She spun around. He dragged her out of the storm, to the outer fringes, and shouted into her ear, "You got any more?"

"What?"

"You got any more strawberries?"

"No! You?"

You're discombobulated
Brain has evaporated . . .

"Wait, there's some." Tenny rushed up to one of the café tables, around which sat several rastafarians finishing off a plate of strawberries. He sneaked his hand in and grabbed a few.

"Hey, mon!" one of them cried.

Tenny ignored him. Bessie came up and said, "C'mon, Tenny, where's mine?"

He gave her a sneer and said, "Piss off." Right away, he devoured the rest.

Gonna be eviscerated
Mangled and emasculated . . .

The club was sweltering. Sweat was flowing as profusely as the beer, and by now most people had stripped down to their soaked t-shirts. People all around Tenny were going from table to table, looking for more strawberries. There were still a few to be had, but the people who had them were uninterested in sharing.

Tenny's stomach rumbled. A strawberry-flavored belch

erupted from his throat. He had to have more.

> *Thank Pigs Incorporated*
> *Pigs Incorporated*
> *Pigs Incorporated*
> *Pigs Incorporated . . .*

Tenny's mouth went dry, and his limbs shook.

When the song was finished and the cheering died down, Fred said into the microphone the band would be taking a short break before starting their second set. Tenny pushed his way through the crowd, to the stage, to catch André before he went down into the dungeon. He grabbed André's arm.

"Tenny! We're a hit tonight, huh? Won't be long till Wax Trax picks us up. What do you think?"

"Hey, stud, are there any more strawberries?"

"Yeah, yeah, don't worry. The man says he has an endless stash. There'll be more coming up for the second set."

"Good deal. How much did this cost you?"

"All of it."

"Are you crazy?"

"Hey, I did it for you, slut. I mean, I knew how much you liked them and stuff, and I wanted some more, too. I thought it would be wild to turn the crowd onto them—"

"But I can't stop eating them. Nobody can. Something's wrong."

"Yeah, sure, I know. I was screwing up all over the place, I had the shakes so bad. I munched a few in between songs, but not enough. Not nearly enough. What, do you think they're laced with LSD or something?"

"How the fuck should I know?"

"Well, what do you want me to do about it?"

"Just get me some more. I think I'm going to pass out or something.

"Sure. We'll be back up in a sec. Sit tight." Then André was gone down the staircase, into the depths.

A tape was now playing over the PA, yet Tenny could hear the crowd's commotion rumbling beneath. No more strawberries were left, and people were getting anxious. It wouldn't be much longer until someone in the club started getting violent.

Maybe it'll be me, Tenny thought as he punched his palm with his fist. He was beginning to get a headache. His mouth was dry, but he knew he wouldn't be able to drink another beer. His stomach knew what it wanted.

They all waited. Most of them smoked one cigarette after another, ignoring their friends and staring into the swirling haze of smoke and damp air. Tenny paced around the club peeking into every corner and eyeing everyone with apprehension. The poseurs were snottier than usual, the punks were growing more paranoid and obnoxious, while the few hippies looked simply stunned. The only people the slightest amiable were some of the rastafarians sitting around a table, eagerly discussing their plans for drying some of the strawberries and smoking them, once they got hold of more.

Sparse applause greeted Mach Twang when they got on stage and started fiddling with their instruments. Fred tuned his guitar and came up to the microphone. "Hi," he said. "There'll be more strawberries coming up."

The crowd whooped and hollered.

Someone shouted, "When?"

"They're coming, so just hang on a minute! Travis wrote

this one: 'Enema of the State.'"

The band started playing, but they weren't playing very well, and no one semeed to care one way or the other. The people on the floor were just milling about nervously, uninterested in slam-dancing. Few people paid any attention to the band. Tenny noticed they kept losing the beat, perhaps distracted by what was going on in the club, or perhaps because they needed more strawberries themselves.

The crowd started booing and hissing, and then it rose into a huge uproar.

"Fuck you!" shouted one woman, over and over. "Fuck you, Mach Twang! Fuck you!"

The band members looked anxiously at each other, confused and angry. They faltered. Gene lost the bass line entirely, and when he reentered, he was off a few beats. André's drumming wasn't steady, Fred kept hitting wrong chords, and all of this clashed with Travis's mostly preprogrammed synthesizer tracks.

"More strawberries!" someone yelled. Then, everyone was up on the floor, crowding in close to the stage, their fists raised. Many were still booing. A few were locked in small scuffles with one another, getting bruised and battered. They all demanded more.

Tenny was still shaking when he saw the Strawberry Man appear from out of the dungeon. No one else seemed to notice him, their attention focused on the stage—but then none of them knew who he was, anyway. He was dressed exactly as he had been the other times Tenny had seen him, and he was smiling.

Two punks rushed up onto the stage, heading for Fred. Just as they did, the band stopped playing, and André stood up from behind the drums and shouted into his own microphone, "Stop!" He pointed at the Strawberry Man. "Look over there, that's the guy who brought the strawberries. If you want more, talk to him! We're fucking through with this shit!"

André, Fred, Gene, and Travis walked off the stage and were enveloped by the closely packed crowd. Tenny was so eager for more strawberries that he paid no attention to where André was—and he didn't really give a shit.

All eyes shifted to look at the Strawberry Man as his rotund figure climbed up the steps, onto the stage. Much commotion arose from all around the club, but when the Strawberry Man stood at the center and looked out over the people, they all abruptly went quiet. He grabbed Fred's microphone from its stand and held it in his flabby fingers.

Feedback squawked before he began. "So, you like my strawberries?" he asked.

The crowd cheered, and some shouted, "More!" as they would have done to get the band to do an encore.

"Oh, there's plenty more where the first batch came from, believe me. And you're welcome to all you can eat. André was quite generous with his money."

Everyone broke out into cheers and applause, waving approving fists in the air.

"Children," the Strawberry Man said, his voice sounding like thunder over the powerful PA system, "I think the second batch is ready now."

Tenny watched closely as the Strawberry Man removed his sunglasses. Behind the pale eyelids, where his eyeballs should have been, there were instead two ripe strawberries, bright red and glistening. He laughed through his rotting, pink teeth, grinning like a madman. Then he removed his hard-hat. Beneath, he was missing his skull cap, and his brain was replaced by a pile of fat, juicy strawberries. As they started spilling out, Tenny thought they looked even more perfect than the ones he had devoured so rapturously the night before. The Strawberry Man bent over, as if taking a bow, and strawberries began streaming out of the top of his head in a seemingly endless flow, cascading over the people and onto the floor.

The crowd scrambled after them.

Tenny shoved his way through the chaos to the center, and ate every strawberry he could get his hands on. They were fantastic.

The Strawberry Man kept on laughing.

Sweet Chariot

(with Catherine Cooke)

———

Kate didn't understand very much about Burial. She didn't know why it was done or what it was for. All she really knew for sure was that she wanted to be Buried more than anything else in the whole world.

Kate's best friend Suzie knew everything about Burial, but she wasn't allowed to tell her yet. She was three years older than Kate and had been to hundreds of them; being around Suzie was the next best thing to being at one herself.

One day more and it would be Kate's eighth birthday. Then she would learn everything. She had been excited all day just thinking about it. The idea of going to a Burial on her birthday was going to keep her from getting any sleep at night, but that didn't matter. At least she would be smiling while squirming around in bed.

"Earth calling Kate! Earth calling Kate!" said Suzie, trying to be funny.

"Uh-huh?" said Kate. They were in her backyard, Suzie

standing behind her while she crouched on the patio. Kate was looking at all sorts of little birds drinking from puddles of rainwater on the back lawn and trying to hold the B-B gun steady. It was easier to keep it still while sitting down, the barrel resting on her knee.

"Don't fall asleep," said Suzie. "C'mon, shoot! They're going to go away if you don't."

Kate hesitated.

"We can't scare them away if they fly off first," Suzie said. "Don't be stupid."

Kate knew Suzie was just kidding around by calling her stupid. "Are you sure I won't hit any of them?" she asked. She was aiming the gun really low, just like Suzie had told her to do.

"Of course I'm sure. You have to shoot just above their little heads or they won't get scared. They won't hear it if you shoot in the air, because they don't have any ears, right? It's go to go *whoosh!* right over their heads."

"Okay," said Kate. "If you say so."

"Shoot! Quick!"

Kate squinted her eyes, held the B-B gun steady, and pulled the trigger. With a *bang,* the gun kicked back in her hands. She hoped she didn't aim too high because of that.

The birds screamed, fluttering their wings and flying away.

All except one.

"Wow!" said Suzie, rushing to Kate's side. "Did you see that? All those birds took off so fast—they must have been scared to death!" She took the B-B gun from Kate's trembling hands and laid it down on the patio.

Kate was crying. "I killed it!" she screamed. "I killed it!"

"What?" Suzie hopped over to where the bird lay on the grass, turning itself in circles trying to get away. "It's not dead, Kate! Come here and take a look. You just nicked its wing, that's all. Look at it rolling around!"

Kate walked across to Suzie, rubbing the tears from her eyes all the way. "I don't want to see."

"Kate, take a look. It's not going to hurt you."

She took a quick peek at the bird and went back to her crying.

"Kate, listen," said Suzie. "We can give the bird a Burial. It'll be fun! What do you say?"

"Really?" she said, sniffling.

"Yeah, really!"

"I thought you couldn't tell me anything. That's what everyone says. We can't have a Burial. My birthday isn't until tomorrow."

"Look, it won't be a real Burial. You can't have one for a bird. It'll just be pretend. You wouldn't want this birdie to sit here and *die,* would you?"

Kate gasped. "Suzie! Sh!"

"Well, you wouldn't, would you?"

"No! Of course not!"

"Then we have to bury it."

They found an empty box of Sugar Munchies in a kitchen cabinet: perfect to put the bird in. They took a heavy shovel from the garage and dug a small hole underneath the Climbing Tree in Kate's backyard, throwing the dirt in a small pile on the grass.

"Now," said Suzie. "We'll pretend you're the Committee, since *you* chose the bird. Hold the box while I get the bulldozer."

Kate took the Sugar Munchies, balancing the odd weight, still hearing the bird chirping from inside. "It's not going to die, is it?"

Suzie was moving some dirt away from the hole with a Really-Digs Dozer. "No, stupid. If it dies it'll have to go to Hell on a dumptruck."

"Oh."

"There, it's ready," said Suzie, setting aside the bulldozer. "Make a speech about why it gets to be Buried."

She placed the box carefully into the hole and tried to say something. "You were a good bird," she began, stammering slightly. "So we planted you under the tree and now you won't have to go to Hell in a truck."

Suzie pushed the dirt on top of the box until the hole was filled. She patted it down with her hands. Her clothes were a mess from all the dirt.

Kate wasn't crying anymore. She couldn't wait until her birthday.

"DON'T GULP YOUR MILK, DEAR," said Kate's mom absently. Dad had come home, and it was almost time for Mom to leave for her night job at the Mayor's office. Kate put down her glass and munched a carrot instead.

Dad had his serious face on while talking to Mom. "Do you think it's wise for us to take Kate to Frank's Burial, Ellen? You know the rate of demonic possession at Burials is going up—at least among teenagers."

"Frank Greenberg is an intelligent, religious boy. I don't think we have anything to worry about. My only concern is that Kate might cry. I've seen it happen; I wouldn't be able to bear the shame."

"Mom!" said Kate, her mouth full of carrot. "I won't cry, I promise! Suzie and I Buried a bird today, and I didn't cry."

"You *what?*" yelled Mom.

Dad said, "I think we ought to have a talk with Suzie's parents, Ellen."

"Yes, but let's wait a while, Phil. We wouldn't want to upset the Greenbergs on such a happy occasion. Which reminds me—Agnes came by today."

"Strutting like a peacock, no doubt. Saying it proves Frank had good parents," Dad said grumpily.

"I'm glad for them, dear, and you should be, too. You know how difficult it's been for them, with none of their parents making it into Heaven. Why, only yesterday, someone we know died and went to Hell."

"Who?" Dad showed some interest now.

"Our dentist, Charlie Fern! I *knew* there was something odd about that man, the way he looked at me when I was in his chair . . ." She shivered theatrically, her face showing disgust.

"*Fern?* He was a good man, Ellen."

"Obviously not, since he went to Hell yesterday."

"Lazarus Unburied!" he swore. "That's isnane."

"Please! Not in front of Kate!" she said.

"Sorry, dear," Dad said. His voice got softer as he continued. "It just doesn't seem fair. When people like Fern die, it makes me wonder about our own chances, that's all."

Mom stared at her bowl of soup.

"Well!" Dad said, shaking off his dour expression. "If Kate's going to Frank's Burial after all, maybe we can get a new dress for her."

"Phil," Mom said in exasperation. "For goodness sake, it

isn't as if one of *us* were being Buried. Her Sunday dress will do."

Kate wanted a new dress, but it wasn't very important. Soon she would know everything Suzie knew. It would be better than with the bird. There wouldn't be any more secrets left.

HER BIRTHDAY, BURIAL DAY, was a Sunday, so after Church, Mom went to work and Dad stayed at home. Kate jumped rope in the morning before Church, watched TV in the afternoon, and buried fallen leaves in the sandbox just before sunset. Dad wouldn't take her to the park; he just kept telling her to stop whining.

Suzie wasn't at home all day. Her church group had taken a field trip to Hell, on the outskirts of town, where they might even see a dumptruck at work. It wasn't fair. Even though she would be going to the Burial of Suzie's dorky brother this evening, she wouldn't get to see Hell for at least another year. She would never know as much as Suzie.

Finally Mom came home, and they changed and ate dinner and went to Services. Kate didn't really understand the sermon. She had heard some of it before. It was about Lazarus, who was Buried by mistake. He was really a sinful man, and Jesus made him come out again and live until he died. After that story, the minister got into an argument with himself about whether Jesus really died for our sins, like it says in the Bible, or if he was actually Buried.

When it was over, the minister changed into a bright robe, and everyone climbed into their cars and started off in happy procession to Valley View Cementery. Kate bounced up and down in the back seat like a piece of popcorn ready to burst.

The cemetery was brightly lit. Flags blew from invisible lines that extended from the pavilion to the grave. A five-piece swing band, out of tune but enthusiastic, blasted "The Stars and Stripes Forever" over loudspeakers. The people already there were as bright as a flower garden, striped and ribboned and laced and polka-dotted.

"They spared no expense," Dad said drily as he pulled up into the huge, crowded parking lot.

"Hush, Phil, be civil. It's their night, after all."

Kate leaped out the door as soon as the car stopped, not wanting to miss anything. The huge pavilion, a roof on fluted pillars, was becoming full. Kate wormed her way through the crowd to the front, leaving Mom and Dad behind. There was Frank Greenberg cutting the funeral cake with his parents beside him, flashing neon smiles. Suzie stood next to Agnes Greenberg, who was dressed entirely in orange, while Mr. Greenberg looked like a salad, all green and yellow and red.

Kate waved at Suzie, who waved back, smiling. Mom came up behind her and held her hand. "Where's Dad?" asked Kate.

"He's in the back, darling. He likes to give other people a chance to see."

"Oh."

Kate thought the sweat on Frank's face must be the beginning of his halo. It caught the bright lights as he took a heavy, sparkling cup from the minister and drank its contents in one gulp. Everybody clapped and cheered.

"That's the Lord's Drink," whispered Mom into Kate's ear. "It's to keep Satan from getting him during the ceremony."

Everything was so marvelous that it seemed like a TV show. Frank sat down on a gilt throne while the band played

"For He's a Jolly Good Fellow."

Kate got in line with Suzie and filed past him with everybody else. She gave him a smile, but he didn't seem to notice her. He was probably thinking about heaven already. He didn't even look at Suzie when she went by.

"That's how it always is," said Suzie. She tugged Kate's hand and pulled her through the crowd of laughing people, leading her at a run to the edge of the deep, straight-sided grave. The coffin was suspended by ropes at the level where they stood.

"You can see everything from here," Suzie said. "You'll be able to hear when Satan talks."

Kate looked at her wide-eyed. "*Satan?*"

"Yeah! When the coffin starts getting covered up, Satan stomps his feet in Hell because he's losing another soul. Sometimes he cries and screams and says, 'Help me!' all in the voice of the person being Buried. It's neat!"

Kate's eyes shone with anticipation. She clutched Suzie's hand tightly and watched the people approach from the pavilion, led by Frank Greenberg, stumbling a little, with one arm around the minister.

"They all do that," said Suzie. "It's because they're so happy."

"Frank sure looks happy."

Old people crowded around the open coffin, gazing longingly at its padded satin softness. The minister helped Frank lie down. He fit perfectly. Everyone waved flags and handkerchiefs as the lid was shut.

Kate waved her hand, jumping up and down, wishing she had gotten a flag. Part of Frank's wide sleeve was sticking out of the side of the coffin, Kate saw, but no one else seemed to notice. The coffin was lowered into the hole.

The minister raised his hand for silence. The ropes were taken up, and there lay the coffin, far below Kate's feet. She remembered the chirps that had come from the box of Sugar Munchies and wondered if that had been Satan speaking in the bird's voice. With a bright new shovel, the minister dug into the mound of rich, sweet-smelling dirt, which fell onto the coffin lid with a hollow THUD.

A muted noise came from the coffin. Kate hugged herself in delight. THUD. Mrs. Greenberg was congratulated loudly by a group of women with beauty shop hair. THUD. The band, with a fanfare and a drumroll, began to play "Swing Low, Sweet Chariot." THUD. Everyone began to sing. Kate joined in off-key and unsure of the words. THUD. *"If you get there before I do, comin' for to carry me home . . ."* THUD. *"Tell all my friends I'm comin' after you, comin' for to carry me home."*

Kate could still hear the noises from the coffin despite the singing. She bent over to hear better "NO!" Satan said over and over, and "Oh my God, please!"

Why would Satan say *oh my God?*

Then the lid began to open and the dirt slid off. It hadn't been shut completely with that sleeve sticking out. Kate tugged on Suzie's hand. "Look!"

The minister gasped in horror and threw his shovel on the mound. The ladies screamed. Frank Greenberg emerged from his coffin and rose to his feet in the grave. His eyes were wide, staring scared, as if he were having a nightmare. He tried to get out, his hands clawing at the sheer sides of the hole while the crowd screamed and cursed and prayed.

"What's wrong with your brother?" Kate asked.

"Wow, Kate! He's possessed! Look at him!" Suzie said, her eyes beaming.

"Possessed!" The cries came from everywhere.

"Drive out the demons!"

Kate tried to get closer, but all the men were crowding around the grave, pushing her and Suzie to the back. "I want to see," she protested.

"You don't need to see," Suzie said. "I've seen it once before. They have to drive the demons out of his body, so they're pouring kerosene over him. Then they'll light it."

"Demons? Can they hurt us?"

"No. Don't worry—the sides of the grave are too high. The men will burn him up, and the demons will leave. Then Frank can go to Heaven."

KAte shuddered with relief as she watched the flames shoot from the grave, and heard Satan screaming through the mouth, loudly at first, then much softer, then gone.

ON FRIDAY, A MANILA ENVELOPE arrived from the Committee, reading: "To be opened by addressee ONLY." It was for Kate, so she rushed up to her room where she had privacy and opened it.

Inside were eight envelopes and two messy photocopied letters. The first letter read:

> *Dear Friend:*
>
> *This is a chain letter. It is also the most important letter you will ever receive, because it guarantees that you will be Buried!*
>
> *All you have to do is follow these simple instructions!*
>
> *Enclosed you will find eight plain, white envelopes*

*and one blank Burial Acceptance Certificate. Make
a list of seven (y) people you feel most deserve to go
to Heaven. Then, make eight (8) photocopies of the
Burial Acceptance Certificate. Fill out the certificates
in the names of the people on your list, and fill out
the eighth one in your name! Use the envelopes to
mail the Burial Acceptance Certificates—and don't
forget to mail the eighth one to yourself!*

*When you have mailed the certificates, think of
one more person who you think deserves to go to
Heaven. Then prepare a package just like this one and
mail it to that person!*

Don't forget to include:

a) Eight (8) plain, white, legal-sized envelopes

*b) Original copy of the Burial Acceptance
Certificate*

c) This letter

*Mail it in a manila envelope like the one you
received. Write "To be opened by addressee ONLY"
near the address and DO NOT put a return address
in the corner.*

*Remember, it's bad luck to break a chain letter!
And don't forget—the sooner you follow the above
instructions, the sooner you and your friends will get
to be Buried. . . .*

KATE DIDN'T KNOW THE NAME of the man who had signed the
letter, but that didn't matter; she was going to go to Heaven!

Mom called her from downstairs. The phone was for her.
She went into the hallway and answered it on the upstairs
phone.

"Did you get my package?" Suzie asked.

"Yeah," Kate said. "You sent that? Wow, that means—"

"I'm going to be Buried! And you, too! I got my certificate in the mail today, so I figured you'd be getting that envelope. But, hey, I've got to go now. Everybody's all excited around here and everything."

"Yeah, I'll bet."

"See you later, Kate."

"Bye," Kate said, hanging up the phone.

She went back to her room to think. She would put Mom down on her list, but Dad swore too much—he wasn't ready for Heaven. She had so many other good friends that it was going to be difficult to choose. She decided to worry about that later.

She hid the envelopes and letters under her mattress and laid down on the bed, dreaming about the beautiful new dress Dad would buy her for her Burial.

Serostatus

——

A SWAMPY HEAT ENVELOPED Tom as he emerged from the refrigerated multiplex into the midnight of a summer's eve under the starless sky of electric Manhattan. Tired, he negotiated his way around the slow-walkers and loud-talkers along West 23rd Street, blubbering and blowing their noses and debating the genius of the movie's *auteur*. Meanwhile, a new batch of victims was standing on line for the late show, eager to subject themselves to three hours of carnage engineered by the best fakers in the business.

It was another Hollywood go at World War II, with flurries of enemy machine-gun bullets killing random American soldiers with gory efficacy—the ones who asked their pals if they wanted to live forever, the ones who pined for their mothers, the ones who clowned in the face of the Axis, even the hero who planted the flag of democracy on the beach as he bled to death. All of them, all dead—on celluloid. Which was like Bill Gates losing a billion dollars after a down day on

Wall Street—it was all "on paper." This was only a movie, af-ter all, and no movie could ever convey the realities of a war to those who had had the good fortune to be elsewhere.

Tom thought of Eric and felt a blast of air-conditioning from somewhere, but it was gone as soon as it had arrived. Perhaps he was coming down with something. He doubted it; he never got sick. He had passed no open doorways and in fact was walking atop a subway grate, under which a train was passing and blasting him with the heat of Hades.

It must have been so easy in the old days, when all you had to do was go down Below and retrieve your lover, provided you were heroic enough, like Gilgamesh. And if you weren't, you could always hire Hercules to make the journey for you. Deals could be brokered. Pluto was not unreasonable. All was not necessarily lost.

Tom rounded the corner at Eighth Avenue and felt a pang of dread at running the gauntlet this evening. All the young men were out, as usual, hanging around in packs outside of The Break and the Big Cup coffee joint and streaming around the corner from Barracuda. Big muscles and tank tops and tight shorts and bulges and tanned flesh and fresh faces and laughter and eyes sizing you up as you passed. Except that for Tom, the eyes no longer turned his way. The twenty-somethings and thirtysomethings must have seen him in their peripheral vision and known he was too old to warrant a glance, a wounded wolf ignored by the rest of the pack. Tom had become invisible to them, ostracized even here in Chel-sea, where he had lived for twenty years. *Go away, leave us alone, look among your own kind.* Or maybe all they were saying was, *you can look, but don't touch.*

Tom smiled to himself. Truth be told, he cared little whether they looked at him or not. What these boys didn't know was that he no longer had any desire for any of them. They were young and careless; the risks were too great. He had had his wasted youth already, and after that all those years with Eric, and after Eric . . . well, the safest sex was none at all, and if nothing else, Tom was determined to survive, as he had done thus far. Latex from the Malaysian jungle seemed fragile protection against so insidious an enemy. Was it worth realizing afterward that the helmet that was supposed to save your life had failed to stop the bullet?

The grocery store was open all night and Tom needed things, so he went in and grabbed a basket. Skim milk, yogurt, eggs, peaches, zucchini squash, sparkling water, raisin bran, chicken breasts, toilet paper, and a pint of ice cream. Even here, at this late hour, the store had five or six guys in it who were shopping leisurely and cruising each other. They were all younger than Tom and never even noticed him. He walked home down West 20th Street with two bags of groceries, past pre-Civil War townhouses, under the shadowed trees, watching out for sidewalks upturned by old roots and waiting to trip him and his eggs.

Halfway down the block, he saw a vision: a drop-dead gorgeous young man (*what we would have called a* youngman *in the bad old days,* Tom thought), in bell-bottom jeans and black leather motorcycle jacket and black leather boots, who was unmistakably cruising him, leaning against a wrought-iron fence, knee jutting out in Tom's path, unlit cigarette dangling, lips wet and sultry. He was as thin as a wraith but not unhealthily so. His hair, long and full and raven-feathered, glistened with a blue sheen in the light of the streetlamp, and his earthy skin and wide-set cheekbones reminded Tom of a

Native American he had met one night in the meat-packing district and linked up with a few other times—but that was ages ago, before Tom had even moved to Chelsea, when he was still a youngman himself, when this boy would still have been a baby, if he had even been born.

Tom avoided his natural inclination these days to pretend he didn't see him, and went ahead and looked.

"Got a light?" the youngman asked.

Tom gave a startled smile—though he should have expected to be asked for either this or the time—and fished out his Zippo. Lighting the cigarette, Tom noted the vibrant flame's reflection in the boy's black eyes. Remarkable how much he resembled that other youngman from so long ago. The tobacco crackled to life and the smoke wafted up, clouding the distance between them and lending the dark face an ethereal quality.

"Thanks, man," the youngman said.

Tom, feeling very much like an oldman, put his lighter away and made as if to go, but the youngman lifted his chin and raised his eyebrows in invitation. Tom could scarcely believe it.

"Come with me to the docks."

"The docks?" Tom said, thinking, *are you crazy?* Did anyone still go to the docks? Were there still any left? The docks in Chelsea had become a yuppie sports complex, and the mayor was having the Village docks dismantled, he thought. Besides, the police were more vigilant these days than in the seventies. That gig was up.

"Come on, man," the youngman said, reaching out and placing his hand on Tom's fly. "I want you, but not here."

Tom looked around but saw none of his neighbors, either

on the street or peeping out their windows. He would have batted the youngman's hand away if his arms weren't full of groceries.

"I'm sorry," Tom said. "I've got to get home."

"Let me go with you," the youngman implored, rubbing Tom.

"Stop that," Tom said, though he wanted it to go on. But he was damned if he was going to invite this boy in. When you were twenty, you never thought your trick was going to rob you out of house and home, but at fifty, you were wise to this potentiality, especially when this boy was the youngest thing to give you the time of day since . . . well, since before Tom could remember.

"How about it, Dad?"

"I can't. I've . . . I've got a partner, see, and—"

Stop it. He's dead. Eric's dead.

"Oh, really?" The youngman cast a cool eye on Tom, drawing down on his cigarette. He dropped his hand from Tom and dug a small brown vial from inside his jacket. He unscrewed the lid, placed the vial up to his nose, and took a whiff. Amyl nitrate. Poppers. He offered it to Tom, holding it up near his nose.

"No, thanks." Tom hadn't smelled the stuff since 1984. He caught a whiff of it now, by accident, and it took him back—to the Anvil and the Mineshaft and the Everard Baths . . . *Jesus.*

"I want you," the youngman said.

"My ice cream is going to melt. I have to go."

Dejection in the youngman's face. Tom broke away and continued toward home. Sweat was dripping down his back, more a result of the encounter than of the humidity. Why should the kid have looked so disappointed? He could have any guy he wanted. All he had to do was go back the way Tom had come, to the Big Cup or even the grocery store. Tom was sure one of them would take him home or go with him to the docks, if there were any docks left to go to, if they hadn't been Disneyfied like Times Square.

Tom looked over his shoulder to make sure he wasn't being followed, but the youngman was nowhere to be seen. He could not have run away so fast, not without a sound, not in those boots. He had to be hiding behind a stoop. Perhaps spying on him.

Sighing heavily, Tom left his groceries on the sidewalk and went back to look for the youngman and tell him to beat it. He made a quick search of the shadows, around the stoops and the garbage cans and the recycling bins, but found no sign of him. The unfinished cigarette was slowly burning itself out on the sidewalk. The scent of amyl nitrate lingered in the air for a moment and was gone—the scent of the youngman, the scent of Tom's youth, the scent of the promise of sex. He picked up the cigarette to finish it but found it so stale it was putrid.

"Oh, and a Bloody Mary for me," Edwin said, handing the brunch menu back to their biceps-flexing waiter, who perhaps was really waiting to be discovered as an underwear model. Edwin, as if in afterthought, laid three thick fingers on the waiter's hairy forearm and said, "Easy on the blood, hon, heavy on the Mary."

Tom glanced apologetically at the waiter, who was new and had never run into Edwin before. The waiter didn't notice Tom's sympathy but only smirk-smiled to himself as he went to the bar.

That brief contact of Edwin's fingers on the waiter's flesh would stay with Edwin all day and enter his dreams. Edwin worked such moments into his life as often as possible. People thought of him as touchy-feely, but they failed to realize it was no accident. Edwin's mind was always working, plotting his next free grope. That "heavy on the Mary" had likely been rehearsed, along with the hand movement. Edwin had always been thus. He took what he could get, from whomever struck his fancy.

"I would have gone with you. Why didn't you call me?"

"Hmm?" Tom's thoughts were elsewhere. Sunday brunch with his friends had been such a routine for so many years, he sometimes slept through the gossip and the chitchat—even now, when it was down to just him and Edwin. It seemed like only yesterday they had a regular crew of eight or nine on Sundays. One by one, they had been bumped off, like the characters in Agatha Christie's *And Then There Were None.*

"The movie. Supposed to be a lot of cutie-pies in that picture. All running around in uniform and getting all muddy."

"Edwin, they're getting their heads blown off."

"Oh, who cares?"

"There was nothing sexy about that movie. Not unless you like bloody American entrails, or severed manly limbs, or a bullet hole in the middle of a corn-fed forehead."

"That's no excuse for not calling. What else did I have to do last night but watch some Ken Burns crap on Channel Thirteen?"

"It was lousy. You would have hated it."

"Heavy on the Mary," the waiter said, lowering the drink.

Edwin's eyes lit up at the sight of it, with its leafy celery stalk erupting over the top. He gave it one good stir and gulped down a fourth of it. "Love it," he croaked at the waiter, reaching out to stroke his arm again. "Better than Viagra."

The waiter moved out of Edwin's reach and said, "And a regular coffee, black," placing a large sloshing mug before Tom.

"For Mr. Boring," Edwin said, still piqued. The waiter smirked again as he turned away, no doubt thinking how much he hated old queens and promising he would never become like them. No Judy Garland records, no MGM musicals, no *Auntie Mame*, no singing showtunes at Eighty-Eights, no Saturday afternoon Metropolitan Opera broadcasts. Not only that, but he would never lose his looks or die for any reason.

Tom sipped his coffee. It burned his lips. He would have to let it cool down. He watched the condensation drip down the side of Edwin's glass. The bloody Mary looked cool and inviting, but Tom dared not. He should have ordered his coffee iced, but it was too late now—if he called the waiter back, it would only look like he was trying not to be boring. "Seems like you don't want anything to do with me anymore," Edwin said, looking for all the world like Shelley Winters in *A Place in the Sun*, sitting across from Montgomery Clift in the rowboat and saying, "*You wish I was dead*," when he had taken her out on the lake for the express purpose of drowning her.

"Edwin," Tom said, "come on, that's ridiculous."

"You never call, we don't do movies, we—"

"We're having brunch, aren't we?"

"You're only doing it because you have to."

"Who's making me?"

"Ask yourself that."

The waiter came with their food and Edwin ordered another Bloody Mary. This time the waiter kept his distance, which was wise; you never knew where Edwin's fingers would stray next. Once, when Tom went with him to a gay Malaysian restaurant in the Village, Edwin had reached under their waiter's sarong and got his hand slapped. People had stared; Tom had wanted to hide.

"More coffee," Tom said. *Make it black, 'cause I'm boring.*

"You want to know why?" Edwin asked. Tom poked the yolks of his eggs Benedict. *See how they run.*

"Survivor's guilt," Edwin said, mouth full of huevos rancheros. "That's the only reason you still brunch with me."

"That's not true," Tom said.

Though it probably was, in part. Of all the men in their circle, Tom had always liked Edwin the least, and all they held in common anymore was their shared grief for lost friends. Edwin had certainly never liked Eric. Tom ascribed it to jealousy; Tom and Eric had managed to have that long-term, mutually respectful, loving relationship that Edwin had proved himself incapable of. For a long time now, Tom had thought he was still putting up with Edwin out of pity, but perhaps he was right and it was guilt.

"You're embarrassed to be seen with me. I'm fat and ugly and make you uncomfortable."

"Stop it, Edwin." Tom came up with a smile. "Listen, I'm sorry I didn't call you last night, okay? I just thought you wouldn't like the movie, that's all."

"That's nice of you to say, Tom. By the way, I was thinking of going to the Film Forum this afternoon. They're showing

Mildred Pierce and *Craig's Wife*. Care to join me?" *If I do, it'll really be out of guilt,* Tom thought. "I can't. I have to prepare for a presentation for Monday."

"I understand," Edwin said, smiling as if he'd just proven a point to himself. "When did you start working again?"

"Just this week," Tom said, but he couldn't sustain the lie for long, so he changed the subject: "Edwin, do guys still meet at the docks, like in the old days?"

"You're asking me?"

"There was this youngman, last night."

"Youngman?" Edwin laughed. "You're going retro on me."

"That's what I felt like, last night . . . like back in the seventies. This youngman was wearing bell-bottoms, and—"

"Oh, the kids are all into that look these days. The personalized T-shirts are out again, too."

"You're right," Tom said. "Back then, I remember one saying I CHOKED LINDA LOVELACE. The other day I saw one that said CHRISTINA SUCKS, BRITNEY SWALLOWS."

He was cruising me, Tom wanted to say. But it would come out all wrong. Edwin would think he was bragging—or lying to spite him—and he would become jealous and pouty. He would be no help at all in sorting it out.

"What does this have to do with the docks?"

"Nothing," Tom said.

Except I went there once with this Native American, when I was half as old as I am now, and I saw him again last night, and he invited me to join him. He said he wanted me.

"They're being dismantled, if you must know," Edwin said. "New York is family friendly now, like Las Vegas, God help us."

"Good-bye, Sodom," Tom said, raising his coffee mug.

"I'll drink to that."

"Hello . . . what?"

"What, indeed?" Edwin contemplated his glass, the inside of which was coated with a gloppy, tomatoey film.

"Because it sure isn't Paradise." Tom swirled the last of his coffee and downed it. It was full of bitter grounds. "Not by a longshot. Maybe Sodom wasn't so bad. Maybe you and I should have gone up in that pillar of fire with everyone else."

Edwin unscrewed the lid off the salt shaker and, with a look of triumph, dumped its contents into Tom's empty mug.

"No looking back," Edwin said. "They wouldn't want that."

Tom wet his fingertip, stuck it in the salt, and licked it off. It tasted like sex, the way sex used to be.

How do you know? he wondered. *How do you fucking know what they would want?*

TOM OPENED THE FREEZER DOOR and hastened the pint of ice cream out of its niche between the ice cube trays and the vodka, which he could identify by its metallic cap, though the bottle itself was obscured by the encroaching frost of more than half a year. Months ago, Tom had nearly thrown it away, but in the end had let it be, as a reminder that he had slain this particular dragon without any twelve-step program or other hocus-pocus. The desire, or need, had simply abandoned him, sometime after he buried Eric. Still, he had concluded the bottle was not without its utility; he could always chip it out of the ice if Edwin or some other guest *(what other guest?)* came over.

He nursed the ice cream as he entered his study, scooping out spoonfuls and sucking them down without hardly considering. The curtains were sashed open but the drawn shifts glowed with sunlight. Eric, whose bed had been situated parallel to the windows after they moved him in here, had requested the shifts be kept down at all times. They made the light less harsh and he enjoyed watching them billow with the breeze in their random, ghostly way. Even after the last drug cocktail failed and the cytomegalovirus finally finished off his retinas, Eric wanted the windows open whenever possible so that when Tom could not be present, the shifts were there to keep him company with their shadow show. Eric said he could feel their subtle touch on his flesh, even at night, even in the absence of moonglow.

The room was musty now with book dust and cigarette smoke, the result of Tom's efforts to replace the odors of the sickroom. He had moved in his computer, drafting table, and bookshelves after getting rid of the bed and everything else, but he had done precious little work here through the entire winter and spring — mostly pleasure reading and chainsmoking. Realizing now that the room had gone too far in its new direction, Tom placed the ice cream on his computer desk and went to open a window. It held fast from the humidity, but when Tom wrenched it loose, a gust of wind lifted the shift and plastered it against his face.

Freeing himself from it, he felt his breath catch, and a sudden pain in his chest, and a panic as if he were suffocating. But the moment passed as soon as he managed to grab the shift and fix it in the sash. He planted his palms on the gritty windowsill and stuck his head out the window for some air. He had to squint in the bright sun. As he looked at the people walking down below on West 20th, he saw a man leaning against the tree right in front, knee jutting out, arms folded across his chest. His face was obscured by the leaves and their shadows. Still, Tom couldn't help but wonder if it was the youngman from last night, waiting for him, wanting him.

"Hey!" Tom shouted.

Startled, the man moved away from the tree, and Tom caught a flash of his face in the dappled sunlight before the man turned his back on Tom and crossed the street to disappear behind a panel van. It was enough of a glimpse for Tom to realize it was not the raven-haired youth of last night. In fact, the man looked something like Eric—the Eric of fifteen years ago, the Eric Tom had met at Fire Island, the vital Eric, the essential Eric. And that, of course, was impossible, because it was here in this room that Tom had held Eric's hand as he slipped away.

"Wait!" Tom called, and rushed out of his apartment and ran down the stairs. *Please wait. . . .*

When he got outside, he crossed the street to the panel van and saw the man walking leisurely at the end of the block, turning the corner at Eighth Avenue, heading north. Tom ran to the corner and followed through the thick Sunday Chelsea crowd, keeping an eye on the back of that head that looked so much like the back of Eric's—when he had more hair. Tom brushed against people awkwardly as he passed, chanting apologies. It was impossible to run, but he was still gaining ground.

At West 23rd, the man crossed the street carelessly against the light. Tom started across, but a Mercedes blared its horn at him and nearly sideswiped him. He waited at the curb, catching his breath while the cars and yellow taxis passed.

Across the street, the man's head bobbed down the subway steps and vanished from view. At the green light, Tom followed across the street and descended into the lower depths, past the token booth and its sleepy guardian and through the turnstiles, with the aid of his trusty MetroCard, just as a C train was screaming to a halt on the platform. The doors opened and loosed a cargo of sweaty passengers. Tom saw *him* getting on the train four cars up the platform. Having only a few seconds, Tom pushed his way past the off-loaders and hustled inside before the doors shut.

The C train pulled out of the 23rd Street station, heading uptown. The conductor said something unintelligible to that effect over the crackling loudspeaker, adding, "*Nekft fftockhh kirtighorftreech pig fftachion ckhhh.*" Tom squeezed past the straphangers and made for the connecting door. The C train rocked back and forth under his feet. Steeling himself, he wrenched the door open and stepped into the darkness between the cars. The gap was narrow, but it seemed like a chasm. The car jump was a move well practiced by New Yorkers—a five-step thing you did in your sleep, like making your approach bowling—step out, grasp the opposite handle, cross the gap, slide the door open, step in. If you thought too much about it, you were liable to screw up. The train lurched oddly as Tom was crossing, but he was safely in the next car before he had time to panic, as they were pulling into 34th Street/Penn Station. It was nearly impossible to note all of the faces of those who disembarked. All he could hope to do was get to the third car ahead and trust that He Who Looked Like Eric was still there.

Tom thought of the many times he and Eric had been subway companions, usually not speaking much during the ride.

In fact, they were never great conversationalists out of doors, whether dining in a restaurant or shopping on Fifth Avenue. When you knew each other that well, small talk was intolerable. One could always tell when the other was making unnecessary conversation. As they grew older together, Tom and Eric fell into a routine of quiet dinners out, quiet movies, quiet walks, quiet vacations. Ever since moving in together, all significant chat had taken place within the walls of their apartment. Behind closed doors, they talked each others' ears off. Eric was always talkier than Tom, but as his AIDS progressed, it became impossible to shut him up. Although he was a good listener, Tom discovered there were limits to what he could stand to hear. Sometimes Tom felt like clamping his hand over Eric's mouth and holding it there. These were the worst times, when Eric was too sick to get out, when a fine meal or a walk or a subway ride might have contented him.

The C train made three more stops before Tom was able to squeeze past all of the tightly packed passengers and make the three additional car-jumps. As he arrived in the fourth car, they were pulling into the 59th Street station, and Tom caught a glimpse of the young Eric as he rose from his seat and exited the car. Tom pressed his way to the nearest door, excusing himself to everyone, and made it out as the doors were closing, their rubber moldings snatching at his heel. The man was heading out the turnstiles, but twenty people had queued up between them. Tom hoped he could catch up with him outside.

Up top at Columbus Circle, Tom saw him entering Central Park, past the marble statue of a reclining Neptune. Although Tom quickened his pace and the man seemed not to be walking any faster, the distance between them was somehow maintained.

"Hey!" Tom called, getting winded. "Slow down, stop!"

He followed him past the rows of park benches that Tom remembered as cruising grounds when he had moved to the city thirty years ago—but no more. These days, they appeared to be rest areas for rollerbladers. He followed him past the restored band shell, down the steps of the Bethesda Fountain, up the neighboring footpath, across the bridge, up a hill, and past a trickling brook, to where the paths went off in all directions through the densest woods of the park, the Ramble.

"Slow down," Tom called. "I've got to rest."

The young Eric looked over his shoulder and smiled that smile that was so recognizable to Tom, from moments of intimacy, outings on a friend's sailboat, Christmas mornings, New Year's Eves, visits with nieces and nephews. . . .

"Eric?" Tom said.

Eric hooked his finger at Tom and mouthed the words *come on* before taking a fork in the path and vanishing into the woods.

"Eric, wait!"

Ignoring the furious beating of his heart, Tom followed the path uphill to where he had last seen Eric, but there was no sign of him here. Tom breathed in deeply, taking in the moist, acidic smell of the forest, and tried to calm himself. There had to be a reasonable explanation for that smile. If he ever caught up to him, Tom would find he looked nothing like Eric at all, and he would offer an awkward apology. As long as Tom could find him.

Tom heard noises and went in their direction, up a rise and into deeper seclusion. To his right, he found two young-men, the first on his knees before the other. Neither of them was Eric. Not that Tom would have put it past him, in the early days of their relationship. There had been that time at Jones Beach in the early eighties when Eric had promised to be right back, and Tom had gone to look for him some minutes later and discovered him in the bush with whomever had happened along. . . .

Tom quietly escaped farther along the path.

"Hey, mister," came a honey-sweet voice to his left. Tom turned and saw an eighteen-year-old guy with curly blond hair, wearing a red T-shirt with white piping on the collar and sleeves, and block lettering that said I CHOKED LINDA LOVELACE. He was leaning against an acacia with his head cocked to one side, rubbing the faded crotch of his jeans and licking his lips.

"Where did you get that shirt?" Tom asked, stupidly. He remembered the boy — or was projecting a memory onto him. They had met late one night in 1977 *(long before Eric, so why should he care?)* on a bench in Stuyvesant Square and had gone off together into the bushes. He never knew the kid's name, but he never forgot the T-shirt or the look, which was classic chicken.

"Got the time?" The kid acted nonplused, indifferent.

"You can't be the boy that I—"

"Like what you see?"

I . . . no, I don't think so. I don't think so at all. . . .

"Come." The kid jerked his head up, begging Tom closer.

Damp forest leaves cushioned Tom's steps as he approached the tree. Youngmen didn't look like this anymore, even if some of them had co-opted the seventies. This was the genuine article. It really *was* him, unchanged since that night, down to the last freckle. Tom came within inches of his face. The boy's breath was hot on Tom's cheek. The rosy lips parted.

"Kiss me," he said, in a voice that echoed all around. "Or don't you like being kissed?"

Tom leaned over, closing his eyes first, as he invariably did before a kiss. He met nothing but air. His forehead bumped against acacia bark. As he reached for the youth, he opened his eyes and found himself groping the tree. He spun his head around, but the boy had disappeared.

Giggling. He heard giggling in the forest and followed it up the path, and as he drew nearer, the sound metamorphosed into grunts, regular rhythmic grunts of pleasure. Behind a group of trees, Tom found two men, naked, standing at opposite ends of a third, filling him up while they kissed each other. Tom recognized them, though they had been tricks only, from one steamy night an eon ago at the Everard Baths, which had burned down long before Tom first encountered Eric on Fire Island. Tom's salad days. Almost impossible to imagine now that any of it had ever happened. That one night at the Everard, Tom must have had five or more men at various times. And there had been so many such nights, at the Everard and the St. Mark's and elsewhere. Many wee hours in Stuyvesant Square, bar pickups, rough trade in the meatpacking district. Hustlers in Bryant Park. Shady encounters in Times Square movie theater balconies. Midnight love on the rotting timbers of the docks. Lazy afternoons in the Ramble.

Tom had no idea how he had managed, out of all that, to survive, when HIV was all around him and his friends long before the virus had a name, long before even those first cases died. It was akin to charging Omaha Beach on D-Day and heading straight for the German batteries without receiving so much as a scratch. Looking back over his shoulder, all he could see for miles of beach were his dead buddies.

Tom could hear scores of men coupling in the Ramble, near and far, high and low. He wanted to shout at them: *Don't you understand where all this leads? Haven't you learned anything?*

The forest, growing darker by degrees, was suddenly calm and quiet. Tom looked at his watch. He hadn't realized it was so late. He turned back and looked through the trees for the threesome, but they were gone.

If any of them had even been here at all.

"Tom," came Eric's voice from behind him.

Tom pivoted, but no one was there. When he turned back, he could no longer recall from which way he'd come.

"Eric?" Tom called.

Eric, came the returning echo. *Steven, Ray, Bobby, Lance, Mark, Joshua, Richard, Enrique, Alex, Bill, Bernie, David, Frank, Howard, Victor, Umberto, Colin, Rex, Bruce, Lester, Jimmy* . . . and all those guys who had never given him their right name . . . and all those whose names he had never asked. . . .

Tom didn't want to still be in the park once the Sun was down. He picked the steepest downhill path, which soon leveled out and split into three more paths, all darkening. Tom's sense of direction had left him utterly, and this part of the Ramble seemed unrecognizable, dense and overgrown.

"Hey, Dad."

The youngman from last night, the Native American he had known at the docks, was standing before him in the middle path in his bell-bottoms, leather jacket, and boots, a wide smile on his face, cigarette smoldering between his lips. Tom remembered him now, with pleasure and unease.

"What's this about?" Tom asked.

"Come on, man," the youngman said. "I want you."

"What for?"

"We had some good times, Tom."

"Did I tell you my name?"

"Don't be that way."

"You're not there. I see you, but you can't be real."

The youngman didn't answer.

Tom approached him cautiously, holding his hand out to touch him, keeping his eyes open. He fully expected to see his hand pass right through to the other side of the leather jacket. But as soon as he was close enough to smell the smoke and the poppers, the youngman seemed to startle, and he vanished.

His image was replaced by that of an athletic guy in a flimsy tank top and Adidas running shorts running right toward Tom, who had no time to step out of the way. The runner looked up from the trail too late, and they crashed. Tom fell to the ground, dazed for a moment before the pair of tanned, lean arms reached down to grab him and help him to his feet.

"Thanks," Tom grunted, brushing leaves and dirt from his clothes. This one seemed real enough.

"Jesus, I'm sorry," the runner said. "I didn't see you. I guess I was in the zone."

"It's dark." Tom absolved him. *And I've been in a zone of my own for a while.* "Can you tell me the best way out of here?"

"Let me rest a moment, and I'll show you," he said, breathing hard. He bent over and placed his hands on his knees.

"I'll take you out with me."

"I don't want to interrupt your run."

"I was finishing, anyway." He grabbed a hand-towel from his fanny pack and wiped the sweat from his face. "Buy you a cup of coffee? It's the least I can do."

"No, thanks, I'm all right."

"Are you sure?"

Tom thought about it for a moment. Just for a moment.

So now here they were at an outdoor café on Amsterdam Avenue, under the streetlamps, and the breeze kept wafting the scent of the runner's sweat Tom's way, and Tom kept squirming in his seat because he could hardly stand it. *He's only doing this so I won't sue him,* he thought. *Worried he might have caused the old man some harm.* His name was Jasper, and he was thirty-five and a pulmonologist, and he had an elegant, taut body that was all his own, not like the cookie-cutter Chelsea gym-boys Tom saw every day prowling up and down Eighth Avenue. Jasper was talking about his job and its stresses, but Tom was only half-listening.

"You shouldn't do that, by the way."

Tom took his cigarette out of his mouth and said, "What?"

"Smoke," Jasper said.

"Oh, I'm sorry, is it bothering you?" Tom poised the ciga-rette over the ashtray, ready to snuff it out.

"The smoke doesn't bother me. But if only you saw some of the lungs I get in my office. I mean, you really should quit."

"I know I should. But go on, please. You were saying?"

To Tom, it was the radiance of a guy like Jasper that spoke to the heart of the matter. Being gay — or straight for that matter—wasn't about sex. It was about aesthetics, and each person's own different appreciation of what constituted beauty. By which he did not mean that gay men had a stronger aesthetic sense. Not stronger, only different. Tom could look at women and understand that they were handsome and yet never feel *beauty* at that deeper level. Men like Jasper sparked something inside that said *Yes!* Most of Tom's gay friends had defined their lives by sex and their pursuit of it. For Tom, it was enough merely having coffee across from a kind of angel.

"I'm rambling, sorry," Jasper said. "What do you do?"

"I'm an architect," Tom said. "A failed one."

Jasper frowned, concerned. "Why do you say that?"

"I haven't done any work in, what, five years."

"Why not?"

Why not, indeed. Tom was worried about getting into that. It scared most people off. But Jasper was a doctor; he ought to understand about caring for people and the pain it left behind. On the other hand, once you showed your scars, you risked losing whatever beauty you might have had in the other's eyes.

"I quit my job to take care of my lover," Tom said, unable to stop himself. "He had AIDS, and he needed constant care, most of the time, anyway. He had his ups and downs. Sometimes he was well enough to get out, but there were times. . . . You don't really want to hear all this, do you?"

"No, please, go on." Jasper was listening intently.

"There were *many* times Eric was near death, but he always climbed back up. The virus was killing him, the drugs were killing him, and the opportunistic infections. . . . But I'm sure you've treated plenty of pneumocystis cases."

Jasper nodded glumly.

"I won't go into the details of taking care of Eric. I don't want to make myself out to be a martyr . . . which I can't be, I guess . . . not yet, anyway . . . but I mean, some years ago, he was almost dead. He was *ready* to die. He had struggled so long, and he was at peace with the idea of moving on — "

I was ready for him to go, Tom thought. But he could never say such a thing to Jasper or to anyone.

"Then the protease inhibitors became available, and his doctor started him on triple combination therapy, and it was miraculous. He sprang back. The opportunistic infections went away, he gained weight and strength, his T cells went up, his viral load went down. He could go out again, and he started to hope again. We knew better, though. Ten years we had been dealing with it together. Still, the hope was there, and Eric lost some of his bitterness — "

"Was he bitter, really?"

"Sometimes," Tom said, and drank down the last of his coffee. "But it didn't last. Eric grew resistant to the protease inhibitor, and the doctor switched him to another one, and another one, but it didn't do any good. At the end, there just weren't any more drugs available that he hadn't developed resistance to. He slipped way back. It happened real fast. He got CMV and went blind, and then he had pneumocystis again for the first time in ages. And that was it."

"I'm sorry. That must be hard. How are you doing?"

"I'm negative, I'm healthy, I'm fine."

"I mean emotionally. I wasn't prying into your serostatus!"

"I don't mind telling you my status. Nothing's going to happen to me. I'm negative and intend to stay that way."

"Don't take this the wrong way, but when I ran into you in the park tonight, you didn't look so good."

"Thanks a lot."

"You look fine now, but when I saw you, you looked like you'd—"

"Don't say it," Tom said. "But I think I did."

"Did what?"

See a ghost, he wanted to say. He wanted to tell him. He wanted Jasper's help. He needed it, needed help, anyway, and who else could he turn to but Jasper? Edwin would be no use. But if he spoke about it with Jasper, he knew what would happen. Jasper would look at his watch and say he had to get going. He would ask Tom to give him a call, because he might be able to recommend a good psychotherapist.

"It's getting late," Tom said, getting up. When you suspected you were about to be dumped, it was always better to pull a sneak attack. "I'm sorry, Jasper, I really must be going. Thanks for the coffee, though."

"Wait," Jasper said. "Let me at least give you this." He pulled his wallet out of his fanny pack and produced a business card. "If you ever feel like you need to talk, give me a call."

"I will. Thanks."

Just talk, Tom thought. Not "Let's have a drink," or "Would you like to have dinner sometime?" or "I have to see you again!"

That was the problem with beauty: It never saw you.

EDWIN HAD LEFT A MESSAGE on Tom's answering machine: "Tom, if you're there, pick up. Oh, that's right, you're *working.* You probably don't want to be *disturbed* while you're *working.* I'm back from the movies, and I've been invited to a party. Very low-key, men our own age, thank goodness! You don't know the host, but he said I could bring you. He has this fabulous loft in TriBeCa, and he's looking for someone to redo it, and he's loaded. Might be a good gig for you, sweet-cakes. And if not, at least you'd meet some *men!* What have you got to lose? I'll be here until nine. Call me. Or, look, I'll give you the address, it's two-thirty-eight Duane Street. Come on by and tell them I sent you."

Tom grabbed the last of the ice cream out of the freezer, but it was too hard to eat. He left it out on the counter.

The shifts were still billowing in Eric's room. He still thought of it as Eric's, even though he had reconverted it back into his study, and maybe that was part of the reason why his drafting table was gathering dust, why he kept turning down freelance work, why he never bothered to call back his former employers who were begging him to return. It was still Eric's room, where he had breathed his last, and he was everywhere here, even if Tom had tried to cover him up. It was here that Tom had said, "We have to get you to the hospital," and Eric had shook his head and said, "No."

Goddamn you, Eric, for leaving me by myself.

Tom decided he should spend no more time in this room. It had been being here this afternoon that had got his imagination going. Maybe he was having an alcoholic flashback, after being dry for so long. That was possible, wasn't it? To go from drinking heavily to no booze at all, overnight, had been jarring enough. All these months later, couldn't it catch up to his mind and make him see things that weren't there? At one time or another, he had known all of those men; they were stored away in his memory and could be conjured up in his dreams, so why not in a waking dream, when he was worn out from following the one he imagined was Eric? Tom had been winded by the time he got to the Ramble. Not getting enough oxygen. Walking in a daze. The victim of an aging, addled mind.

Sometimes I hate you for being negative, Eric had said to him, at his worst moment, shortly after he had lost his eyesight. *This is never going to happen to you. You're going to find a new boyfriend and live to be a hundred, and someday you'll get Alzheimer's and forget all about me, I'm telling you.*

Tom closed the door to his study and locked it.

He had heard it said that lonely people lived in a world of their own making, that it was they who chose not to make friends. To a certain extent, he believed it to be true. Even after all his friends had died, he had had plenty of opportunities to make new ones. He had met people and made efforts to try to like them. But they all seemed like bad copies of other people he had known. None of them seemed real. The real ones were long gone.

That was why he couldn't go to Edwin's stupid party tonight. Men his own age. That meant men who either were going through what Eric went through *(and I can't handle another Eric)* or were survivors themselves—the unwanted, the prudent, and the just plain lucky. Tom didn't want a friend like himself. He wanted a Jasper, one with youth and beauty and vitality still on his side—as long as Jasper wouldn't die on him. *What are you saying? You don't even know if you'll ever see him again.* Tom placed Jasper's card by the phone and promised himself he would call him tomorrow, after the Sun came up and things looked good again. To call now, while he was depressed, would only make him sound like a pathetic old queen.

I don't want to ever be like that, Eric used to say, when he was young and healthy, when they spotted an elderly gay man on the street. *Like Blondie says, "Die young, stay pretty."*

The ice cream had turned to soup. Tom drank it all, damning his too-high cholesterol, and threw the container away.

He had to get out. The apartment was too gloomy, and in fact he should think about moving. He would never find another rent like the one he was paying—not for a sunny floor-through two-bedroom in Chelsea—but perhaps he should move anyway, up to Inwood or to one of the outer boroughs or to a new city altogether—somewhere far away from all the old memories.

But he couldn't solve that tonight. What he needed was a walk, through Chelsea and the West Village, among the living.

BACK WHEN TOM FIRST MOVED to Chelsea, the Village was still the center of the gay universe, and he might as well have been moving to Poughkeepsie. Some of his friends back then even refused to venture north of the border at 14th Street. Tom had been staking out territory in the land of the Puerto Ricans, who made terrific neighbors and who tolerated him while muttering *maricón* and *loca* and *puta* under their breath. Now Chelsea was all but gay, with its own look that Tom was too old and too soft to fit.

But it was still his city, and these were the manhole covers beneath his feet, endlessly purging steam out into the night air. These were the sidewalks, shared by man and dog and hosed down by Cuban doormen and Mexican busboys. This was the cobblestone street no one had bothered to pave over, the stones roundly polished by a hundred years of motorcars, the Italian workmen who laid them long since laid to rest in rows even neater. That was the Empire State Building peeking over everything, upper floors illumined in Babylonian splendor. The World Trade Center was gone, but it had never really belonged. Edwin was the only one he had ever admitted these feelings to, and that had been a mistake. "I always hated it," he'd told him two days after the collapse. He'd had to get it off his chest, and Edwin was the only person at hand: "It was so permanent, and I knew no one would ever bother to dismantle it, so I used to wish that it would just disappear. And now that it's gone, I feel guilty, as if it were somehow my fault." Edwin had stared at him stupidly without saying anything, and no doubt he had shared this as a tidbit of gossip with anyone and everyone.

Tom tried to catch the eye of a man on Christopher Street—any man—with no luck. He passed two Hispanic youths wearing baggy shorts and baseball caps and earrings, looking like any other barrio boys until you heard them open their mouths, and out came that particular cadence of speech no straight man would ever wish to adopt. There was a fortyyear- old black man in designer duds, with a beautiful face and elegant shoulders, wearing a subtle, sexy cologne, staring ahead, never noticing Tom. And a thirty-year-old white guy in a skin-tight T-shirt, leaning against a wall, smoking a cigarette, obviously looking for someone—but turning away as soon as his eyes met Tom's.

Tom walked to the end of Christopher to West Street, where the cars sped sixty miles an hour or more. This was one street in Manhattan where you genuinely had to wait for the light to change before venturing off the curb. When it was safe, Tom hurried across, toward the broad Hudson River and the docks.

What am I doing here? he asked himself. *Why bother?*

A paved walkway ran along the river here, new within the last five years, stretching from Chelsea all the way down to Battery Park, with a demarcation line painted to keep the walkers on one side and the bicyclists on the other. Even at this hour, some people were hanging out, sitting on benches, listening to boom boxes, doing figure-eights on rollerblades, laughing, touching, enjoying each other's company.

Tom walked north, toward the old docks. The lights along this stretch of the walkway were apparently burnt out and he saw no people here. Tom leaned against the waist-high concrete barrier at the river's edge and looked out over the dark waters reflecting the lights of Hoboken across the way. He followed along the barrier to what was once Pier 49 or Pier 50 or Pier 51—how was he to know? They were crumbling, closed off by chain-link fencing and signs in red paint: WARNING—DANGER—KEEP OUT. If the mayor was dismantling them, Tom saw no sign of it—no cranes, no heavy equipment, no waste bins filled with debris.

Human debris, he thought, and distinctly heard Katherine Hepburn's voice saying it—just another voice in his head.

"Hello again."

This wasn't in his head. It was from the Native American youngman whose hair was black as night. He was sitting on the concrete barrier, where a moment ago no one had been. He looked down at Tom and offered him a comely smile.

"Who are you?"

"You know who I am," the youngman said. "If you mean

what's my name, isn't it a little too late to ask?"

"What are you doing here? What do you want from me?"

"I told you already. I want you."

"I don't get it. Did Eric send you?"

The youngman shrugged. "Who's Eric?"

Someday you'll get Alzheimer's and forget all about me. Tom was too young for Alzheimer's—at least he thought so— but he wondered if he was experiencing some kind of dementia. His grandfather had seen people who weren't there, had carried on conversations with them, had watched football with them in his living room in Ohio, because of his dementia. Things like that ran in families, it was certainly possible, but then again. . . .

"Can you climb this?" the youngman asked, indicating the tall chain-link fence behind him, beyond the concrete barrier. On the other side of the fence stretched a decrepit wooden pier.

"Eric's angry because I've outlived him, is that it?"

"I told you I don't know any Eric. Come on, follow me."

With that, the youngman swung his legs over the other side of the barrier and dropped down. He gripped the chain links and began climbing, seemingly without effort. But he was young.

"Come on!" he called when he reached the top.

"I don't know if I can," Tom said, but he found that he wanted to. He had to know what it was all about.

"You can do it, Dad. It's easy."

Tom found it difficult enough getting over the concrete barrier. Once at the fence, he looked to see if he could find a gap, someplace where someone had cut the wires—but no. If he wanted to know, he would have to go over. *Come on,* the voice urged in his head. *It's easy.* He had climbed fences like this plenty of times when he was young. It couldn't be that hard. He breathed in deeply and grasped the fence. He put one hand over the other and was able to stick the toes of his sneakers into the holes to help himself up. He had to go up a ways and rest, go up a ways and rest, but at last he was at the top, precariously.

The youngman was gone. He must have made his way down the other side. The pier below was too dark for Tom to see him.

"Hey you, get down from there!"

A voice from behind him—sounded like a cop—but Tom didn't look around. Too late to go back. The youngman wanted him. *Come with me to the docks,* he had said last night. *Come.*

Tom threw one leg over the top, and, maintaining a tight hold, managed to get the other leg over but scrambled desperately for a foothold. The fence was wobbling and swaying with his weight. One hand lost its grip. His feet found no purchase. He was hanging on by four fingers. He was just about to fall when he snagged the toe of one shoe in the fence and grabbed on again with his other hand. He stayed there for a mo-ment, catching his breath while his heart beat fiercely. He felt very old up here.

You took the last years of my youth, Tom thought—not for the first time. He had said it before, aloud, one day when he had utterly exhausted his supply of patience and compassion. He had said it to Eric, as he lay dying. *Look at me, Eric. I gave up the best years of my life being with you and taking care of you. Staying true to you has kept me from being true to myself. It's not the life I wanted. I want to be out there hav-ing fun. I feel like I'm in a cage. . . .*

If he didn't get down, he might lose his grip and fall to his death. He drummed up his courage, closed his eyes, and be-gan his descent. He went down hand over shaky hand, find-ing holes for his toes, while the fence warped and rattled.

He made it down to safety. The cars zoomed down West Street beyond, oblivious to him. He looked for whoever had told him to get down, but he saw no one along the walk-way— no one at all.

"Youngman!" Tom didn't know how else to call for him.

There was no way off the pier except to go back over the fence, and Tom wasn't ready to try that again. The three oth-er sides dropped off into the Hudson River, and he didn't feel foolish enough to jump in. He was stuck over here, and for what?

Desperation. You're so desperate, you'd pursue sex with someone you screwed a quarter century ago on this dock and who must be dead, or he wouldn't be coming to you. . . .

"Youngman?"

The water lapped against the piles.

"I'm out here," came the youngman's voice from the end of the pier, which was nothing more than a void extending into the subtly glimmering Hudson.

Venturing farther out seemed unwise. He could fall through an unseen hole and land on the rocks under the pier. The whole structure could collapse and take him with it. It was unsafe.

"Here, I'll help you," said a honey-smooth voice in his ear.

Tom turned with a start to find the blond youth beside him,

the one with whom he had gone into the bushes at Stuyvesant Square, the one with the bragging T-shirt.

"No," Tom said. "I want to go home." "Why?" the blond asked. "No one wants you there. You don't have any friends on that side. We're all over here. Come."

"But there's Edwin—and . . . and Jasper—"

"You hate Edwin," the blond said.

"Jasper doesn't love you," said the raven-haired young-man.

"We're the only ones who love you."

"That's right. See for yourself."

As Tom's eyes adjusted to the darkness and he looked more closely, he saw that the pier was not made of worme-aten wood after all. The entire length and breadth of the pier was teeming with sweaty male bodies slithering one atop the other like slippery seals basking in the sun, arms reaching out, hands caressing, legs contorting, backs arching, mouths meeting, buttocks rising. . . . It was hard to tell where one body began and the next ended, or whether they all made up a single, writhing mass. They made a humming, hungry drone of a sound.

Looking behind him toward West Street, Tom saw Eric standing on the other side of the chain-link fence, looking not a day older than that first day on Fire Island. It was easy to see why Tom had fallen for him. He had always been a dish.

"Eric!" Tom grabbed the fence and shook it.

All he wanted now was to get back to the other side. He didn't have to stay. He could climb back over, if he tried. Maybe that was what Eric wanted, and he was merely testing Tom to see which side he would choose.

"Eric, stay there. Please! Wait for me!"

Tom reached for the fence and began to climb. The raven-haired youth and the blond grabbed at him, but he pulled loose. The mass of men pressed up against the fence, reaching their arms toward the sky. Tom made it to a few feet below the top before he had to stop to catch his breath. He couldn't, though. It was shallow, too shallow, and he felt light-headed. A sharp pain shot up his left arm, and it felt as if someone kicked him hard in the chest. He let go and began to fall, calling Eric's name.

AFTERWORD

———

"After You've Gone" first appeared in Michele Slung's anthology *Stranger* (HarperCollins, 2002) and was subsequently selected to appear in *Best American Mystery Stories 2003* (Houghton Mifflin, 2003). In my note that accompanied the latter appearance, I expounded in some detail about its relation to a common theme in my work, which is the often predictable eruption of violence that occurs when some men are confronted with sexually confusing predicaments. Witness my novel *The Chimney Sweeper* for a further exploration of this.

"A Doll's Tale" has a provenance that I believe to be obvious owing to the ubiquity of trashy horror novels about demon dolls. It was a natural idea to look at it from the doll's point of view and to try to find out how demon dolls end up that way in the first place. Although this tale has no overtly gay theme to it, the doll's voice has a bitchy tone that I confess I was unaware of while I was writing it. *Hmm.*

"The Penitent" was written in response to an invitation to contribute to the anthology *Dark Love,* in which indeed it first appeared. When I received the invitation, the working title of the anthology was to be *Blood Lust,* and it appeared there would be no boundaries as to subject matter. This tempted me to push the boundaries of taste as far as I could go, and perhaps veered into sacrilege, although you can be the judge of that. (In its own way, this story is quite devout!) *Dark Love* also contained an original Stephen King story that helped perpetuate multiple international editions and translations in numerous languages. However, when *Dark Love* was published in Germany, the publisher had "The Penitent" removed, as they felt that it might get them sued for corrupting the morals of German youth. What a badge of honour!

"The Naked Tooth" was published in the gay literary journal *Christopher Street* not long before that journal's demise. I had been reading *Christopher Street* since I was fifteen years old, in bound editions at the Coe Library of the University of Wyoming, and was thrilled at being published in the same journal that had published short fiction by the likes of Felice Picano, Ethan Mordden, Andrew Holleran, Robert Ferro, Edmund White, James Purdy, and Tennessee Williams (whose last tale, "The Killer Chicken and the Closet Queen," appeared in *Christopher Street,* and whose first, "The Vengeance of Nitocris," was published in *Weird Tales*!).

"The Cat's Meow" was my first sale and first published story, appearing in *Eldritch Tales.* I had met the editor, Cirspin Burnham, while we both stood on a lengthy queue at Archon 12 in St. Louis, in 1982, to obtain Stephen King's autograph on our copies of his books. We spent a good two or three hours in line, and had a great conversation about Weird Tales, H. P. Lovecraft, Stephen King, and other topics. Crispin encouraged me to send him a story, and a year later, in 1983, I did. It took another three years for it to make it through the Eldritch Tales backlog and appeared in issue No. 12 in 1986.

"Spoiled Rotten" was my second tale to Crispin, and appeared in *Eldritch Tales* No. 28, in 1993. There is something about the tale that I like after all these years, although it is little more than a pale variation of "The Outsider" by H. P. Lovecraft and innumerable other variations by divers hands.

"Telling Tales" is another variation on a theme, this time derived from "The Tell-Tale Heart" by Edgar Allan Poe. All I considered was what would happen if the murderer who narrated Poe's tale were to be put on trial for his crime, in the modern day and age of circus-like show trials and *Court TV*. Naturally, I gave the story my usual gay bent as well, since I've always wondered just exactly what the relationship was between the narrator and the old man he lived with. . . .

"The Strawberry Man" came about by invitation of the late Eric Garber, a pioneering gay anthologist who also co-edited the seminal *Worlds Apart* collection of gay science fiction stories for Alyson. Eric was assembling an all-original anthology of gay horror stories and asked me for a contribution. My tale reflects my teenage interest in punk and new-wave music and my desire to present a young gay couple who didn't fit the usual stereotypes, being down-at-the-heel skateboarders rather than well-to-do sophisticates. The Strawberry Man himself was inspired by a real person I encountered one day in rural Wisconsin, peddling strawberries off the tailgate of his pickup, wearing overalls and a shiny aluminum hardhat . . . and who struck my imagination as terribly creepy, although he was probably harmless.

"Sweet Chariot" is a collaboration with my sister Catherine Cooke (a/k/a Catherine Montrose), and one of my earliest tales. It began with my own version (originally entitled "Mature Burial") and although the concept was unique, it didn't quite make it as a story. Catherine said, "Let me have a go at it" . . . and then we revised it jointly before sending it around for publication. We were delighted to see it published in Gordon Linzner's *Space & Time*.

"Serostatus" is another tale that stewed for a very long time in my mind before emerging onto the page. I used to live in Manhattan and, as a gay man who arrived there in the 1990s, felt haunted by the ghosts of those who had come before me and who had been blindsided by HIV/AIDS before anyone knew how to protect themselves. I was trying to capture the romantic freedom of the 1970s and juxtapose it against the ultra-cautious Tom trying to wall himself off from the world while living with significant survivor's guilt. The comparison of the HIV/AIDS experience to losing loved ones in wartime reflects my personal feelings about it and a general resentment that I share with Tom about the continued general level of public apathy. I was quite proud to see this story published in *The Magazine of Fantasy & Science Fiction*, where so many of my literary heroes had been published before me, from Richard Matheson to Fritz Leiber to Charles L. Grant to Stephen King to Robert Silverberg. Not that invoking those names here will ever help me reach their lofty status!

THE RAPE OF
GANYMEDE
A Greg Quaintance
Novel
$18.00

From the author of *The Chimney Sweeper* and *Torsos* comes a novel of a gay private eye working the mean streets of New York City's Chelsea circa 1998.... Greg Quaintance sports a Desert Storm tattoo, packs a Glock, and drives a Plymouth Barracuda, but only those who know him best see the wounds etched in his heart. As a P.I. in Manhattan's Chelsea neighborhood, he is hired to thwart an extortion attempt aimed at Jimmy Gilbert, a billion-dollar man-child musical superstar accused of having sexual relations with a teenage boy. But when Gilbert's accuser turns up dead and the boy goes on the run, the bodies of the rich and not-so-famous start piling up. From the canyons of Manhattan to the halls of presidential power, Quaintance must now penetrate a minefield fused with greed, depravity, and violence.

THE FALL OF
LUCIFER
A Greg Quaintance
Novel
$18.00

Greg Quaintance, the gay and brooding prvate eye hero of John Peyton Cooke's *The Rape of Ganymede*, returns to investigate a dark new mystery set in New York City, circa 1998.... When a distraught father hires Greg to find his missing son, Greg finds himself up to his neck in the world of the 1990s Goth club scene. But that's the least of his troubles. It's a case so bizarre, it might lead Greg to start believing in vampires.... Greg Quaintance, a Gulf War veteran with a Desert Storm tattoo, is no stranger to blood ... but only those who know him best see the wounds etched in his heart.